D0562468

TEA IS FOR TERROR

A Claire Gulliver Mystery

Also by Gayle Wigglesworth

GAYLE'S LEGACY,
RECIPES, HINTS AND STORIES CULLED FROM A
LIFELONG RELATIONSHIP WITH FOOD

TEA IS FOR TERROR

A Claire Gulliver Mystery

by

GAYLE WIGGLESWORTH

To Janice

Enjoy!

Gayle Wigglesworth

Library of Congress Control Number: 2004094719

ISBN: 0-9741685-2-1

Koenisha Publications, 3196 – 53rd Street, Hamilton, MI 49419
Telephone or Fax: 269-751-4100
Email: koenisha@macatawa.org
Web site: www.koenisha.com

This book would not have been possible without the support of my husband, David, who shares my travels, who believes in me and has always encouraged me. And I would like to thank my daughters, Janet and Danielle who were fearless editors.

I dedicate this book to all those people who have a dream and refuse to give it up. The fact that you are reading this book demonstrates that dreams do come true.

"He's sending me to Club Med."

Claire watched the pasty face pale even further as he nervously resumed chewing on his ragged cuticle. She felt her resolve slipping.

"We're leaving Saturday you know," she said gently.

That didn't seem to daunt him.

She tried, "We'll be gone fourteen days."

He just looked pathetically hopeful.

"Well," she sighed, "I can't promise you anything but I'll try. Look, why don't you browse through the books while I see what I can do."

She headed for her office tucked in the back of the store, eyes automatically checking every detail as she passed. The tall shelves along all the perimeter walls were clearly labeled and colorfully filled. The low back-to-back shelves, set strategically in the middle of the floor, invited browsing. Here and there sat benches and wooden chairs just like the public libraries had when she was a kid. She passed the alcove and noted it was neat, inviting the serious trip planners to spread out their selections on the tables for a closer look. And its scattering of old sofas and overstuffed chairs allowed a comfortable place for customers to carefully peruse books they were considering for purchase.

She couldn't help her proud smile. And why not, she thought. Gulliver's Book Shop, slightly worn, comfortably attractive, was her contribution to the community.

"Sucker," Mrs. B whispered as Claire passed.

Claire agreed. They were leaving Saturday. Everyone had paid six weeks ago. They had already had two orientation meetings to prepare for this adventure. So why was she even thinking of adding another person to the group?

Because somehow, instead of just being pathetic, Arnie White was appealing. And she understood why he would rather go with Lucy Springer than spend two weeks at a posh Club Med. Since the travel agent had apparently hinted to him that if he talked to Claire or Lucy they might let him join them even at this late date, he had been pounding on the door of the bookshop before she even opened.

She punched in Lucy's number first but only got her answering machine. She knew when Lucy was writing she just let the machine answer, so Claire reluctantly left a message. Obviously, Lucy wasn't going to give her an easy out by making the decision on this one. Next the travel agent, who could hardly hide her glee at the prospect of another commission, but she eagerly confirmed she could obtain another seat on their flight, albeit at a higher price.

The only other real obstacle was accommodations. There was no way she could ask Rosa, Lucy's assistant, to contact all the hotels to arrange additional accommodations. But Claire had an idea about the solution to that problem. She sorted through her file for the trip.

There it was. The form she was looking for, Warren Grey.

There were only two unattached males on the trip but crusty Joe Onerato had insisted on his own room. That left Warren with a single, too. All the rooms they booked were really doubles, so a single occupant paid twice as much for the room. That was why Warren was disappointed that Joe didn't want to share and thereby reduce their costs.

She quickly punched in his work phone number. "Warren, this is Claire Gulliver. Can you talk a minute?"

"Sure, just trying to clear my desk before vacation. Nothing's wrong is there?"

"No, no, everything's set. I don't know about you but I'm getting pretty excited. I've already started packing. You know, checking to see if it will all fit in my bag." She laughed at herself.

"Me, too. Uh, excited, I mean, not packed." He paused; the truth was that he alternated between excitement and disappointment. As great as this trip sounded it wasn't what he preferred. He really wanted to vacation with his son for two months, as he did every summer. But Carol, his ex-wife, tried to explain that Ryan was growing up. It wasn't that he didn't love him anymore. It's just at this age the boy would rather spend his time with his friends than in California with his Dad. So, thanks to that early warning, by the time Ryan got up enough nerve to suggest he come for only one week this summer, Warren was prepared to discuss it with some understanding, keeping his own disappointment hidden. And since then he had made a point of telling Ryan about the great trip he was going on, so Ryan wouldn't feel guilty. But he really signed on for this trip to help fill the time he suddenly was going to have on his hands.

Claire, unaware of Warren's ambivalence launched into to her pitch. "Warren, are you still interested in having a roommate and getting half your hotel fees refunded?"

"Well, uh... sure. Who?"

"His name is Arnie White and he's desperate to come with us. He's one of those computer types. He works down in Sunnyvale, not far from your office.

"He doesn't really want a vacation, because he's all wrapped up in his job and his computer. But when he had his annual physical the doctor said his blood pressure was too high and he needed to take a vacation. Well, his boss is determined that he follow the doctor's recommendation. He's apparently just too valuable to risk, you see? In fact his boss thinks so much of him he signed him up for Club Med, as sort of a bonus for the work he's done. And Arnie is in a panic that he'll have to go.

"So," she hurried on, "he could go with us if it didn't mean rearranging all the rooms we've already booked. And I remembered that originally you wanted to share."

She paused for just a minute to let it all sink in. "I know it's last minute, but I think you'd get on with him. He seems very nice. Kind of reserved, you know, and probably about your own age."

Warren had a sudden vision of himself at Club Med, shuddering at the thought of his too thin body in a bathing suit amidst the brawny and beautiful people they had pictured in their ads.

"Would you be willing to meet him?" Suddenly Claire realized she was pushing Warren and immediately contrite, she backed off a bit. "Warren, if you'd rather not, just say so and I'll tell him no. He's not going to know. He probably doesn't even expect us to take him, asking at the last minute like this."

"No, no, I don't need to meet the guy. If you think he's okay then it's fine with me. And I won't mind getting some of my money back."

Claire smiled. "Thanks, Warren. I appreciate it. And I'm sure Arnie will. I'll let you go now, see you Saturday morning."

She called the travel agent back, arranging for her to take care of Arnie's fees, assuring her that she would have Lucy make sure the changes were communicated to the British tour company.

It seemed like it took forever to finish the details and get the grateful Arnie out of the shop so she could get back to the work she had planned for the day. At least Mrs. B was in today so she could rely on the shop running smoothly, allowing her to make some progress on the stack of work that had to be completed before she left.

Thank goodness for Mrs. B. Claire smiled to herself remembering the day Mrs. B announced she would take the job Claire had posted on the window.

Gulliver's Travels Bookshop sat on a side street in the upscale little town of Bayside on the San Francisco Peninsula. Her father's Uncle Bernie had owned it since coming home from the war, in the Forties. In the latter years of his life the store had become as run down as he had, the books outdated, the store dusty and musty smelling. And when Uncle Bernie passed away in his sleep one night he had left the store, the little cottage, four blocks away and his prized 1953 Cadillac convertible to his one remaining relative, Claire Gulliver.

She had been stunned. Somehow it had never occurred to her that she would receive Uncle Bernie's largest. Perhaps she expected him to live forever, as he seemed very old for as long as she had known him. But inheritance had come at a good time for her. She was recovering from a traumatic experience and felt the need to make some major changes in her life. The inheritance became the catalyst. Within months she had given up her career in the San Francisco Library system, withdrew her pension and all her savings, moved to the Peninsula and somehow transformed the bookstore into a cozy haven for travelers and would-be travelers.

That first year in the shop had been impossible. Fortunately she didn't know it then, and so she just worked harder, spending almost every waking hour at the store. Then in her fourteenth month she broke even, covering her expenses from her sales. From that point on she could start adding improvements. She sponsored a lecture series, and she invited travel authors to book signing parties. The shop soon became known as *the place to visit* before any trip. No destination was too remote or exotic for Gulliver's. That's when Mrs. B arrived to rescue her.

Mrs. B, Betty Jo Bianci, was a local. She lived only a few blocks away and knew almost everyone in town. She was short and energetic. Her face was heavily creased with the lines of living, and Claire thought her age was somewhere between an old fifty-five and a young seventy-five. She looked like grandmothers did in the movies when Claire was a child, not like the glamorous, perpetually young, grandmothers looked now.

Mrs. B said she needed the job desperately, not because of the money but because she said she wasn't ready to get old, which was the only choice she had unless she did something about it. Mrs. B could have been one of her mother's friends. But while her mother was cautious, always worrying and fretting about what could happen, Mrs. B tried new things and swore risk was the tonic of life. She was always challenging Claire to live life to the limit. She was even teaching Claire to play poker, appalled at her lack of education.

Hiring Mrs. B was one of Claire's better decisions. Mrs. B loved the shop, almost as much as Claire did. And she was touchingly grateful when after the first year, Claire insisted she have the title of Assistant Manager, and of course, a small portion of the shop's profits. With Mrs. B's support Claire could make dental appointments, get her hair cut occasionally, and go to book shows without fits of panic about what was happening at the shop. And Claire could agree to participate in Lucy Springer's *Untour for Armchair Adventurers* instead of just sponsoring it.

Despite her rambling thoughts, Claire had made real progress on her To Do list when Mrs. B called, "Claire, Rosa's on line two for you."

Claire picked up the receiver, glad for the chance to finish the arrangements for Arnie. "Hi, Rosa. Thanks for calling. Did Lucy tell you we added someone to the tour?"

"No, no, I didn't know. I'm calling for a different reason. Miss Gulliver, I'm afraid I have bad news." Rosa's stiff, formal words caused a quiver in Claire's abdomen.

"What's the matter?"

"It's Mrs. Springer. She's had an accident."

"An accident? What kind of accident? Is she hurt? Where is she?"

"She's at the hospital. She took a rather nasty spill down the back stairs and broke her leg. They just set it. The doctors say she has to stay in the hospital for a couple of days. Then they'll cast her and release her."

"But, we're leaving Saturday."

"Well, I'm afraid Mrs. Springer is not. The doctors were adamant."

"Oh, my God! Lucy can't go?" Claire was stunned. Lucy couldn't go! Lucy had an accident?

Then she was ashamed. "Oh, Rosa, poor Lucy. How is she? Is she in a great deal of pain?"

"Not now that they've given her something. But it was pretty bad. I didn't know what to do; at first I thought she was dead." For once the stoic Rosa sounded shaken.

"Thank God, you were there. How did it happen? I just can't imagine her falling down the stairs."

"It was something about that neighborhood tomcat going after Fluffy. She raced out to get the garden hose to chase him off and apparently one of the steps broke. Somehow her leg got caught in the railing when she fell. That was a blessing, because while it did do rather vicious damage to her leg, it's probably what saved her from landing on the cement."

"She could have been killed." Claire shuddered. "I don't even want to think about that. Where is she, Rosa? I'll come over right now."

"We're at Sequoia, but no sense in rushing down. The doctor sedated her and they don't expect her to come out of it until this evening. I know she wants to see you. She kept moaning about the trip. She wanted me to call you right away but I just couldn't leave her until now.

"But she's most anxious to see you. So if you could come by this evening, say about six, I'm sure it would be a comfort to her."

Claire shook her head as she hung up, noting the tremor in her hand. Lucy was worried about the trip. Wasn't that just like her? She almost killed herself but she worried about them.

Lucy Springer was a rather popular writer of travel books on Great Britain. Claire had agreed to host an event one evening at Gulliver's promoting Lucy's most popular book, *Daffodils in the Cotswold's.* She and Lucy had become fast friends.

Lucy had a darling house in a posh neighborhood of Burlingame, located up against the hilly terrain of Hillsborough, not too far from Bayside. Lucy and her gardener had managed to create a breathtaking garden out of the steep hill that was her backyard. It started with a small deck off her kitchen and then a series of steep stairs ending up on a stone and cement terrace. There she kept some comfortable lounge furniture, then more terraces with a meandering path to the little stream, which cut across the bottom. Everywhere you looked were shade trees and beds of flowers. Claire loved to sit there and watch the birds enjoy the birdbath and Fluffy, Lucy's enormous Persian cat, chase butterflies while Lucy, who couldn't sit and enjoy it, weeded or planted or thinned, anything to get her fingers in the dirt. The first time Claire saw the garden she told Lucy to forget the gardens in England she was always writing about, hers was worth a whole book. Lucy just laughed at her.

But those damn steps had nearly killed Lucy.

Lucy was older than Claire, sophisticated and fun. She had been married twice and now said she was single to stay. She totally understood Claire's absorption in her business feeling the same about her writing. The difference was Lucy had time to play after her book was at the printers and before all the publicity and personal appearances were required to market it, while the demands on Claire were constant.

Lucy couldn't believe Claire was able to create such a haven for travelers when she had never even been out of the country, in fact had traveled very little even inside the United States and that mostly connected to her business needs. Lucy was determined to help Claire rectify that gap in her life. This trip was going to teach Claire and the rest of the group to travel on foreign soil. If Britain could be called foreign. And Lucy insisted they would all notice how different it was from the United States. But now they couldn't go.

"Claire, you look rather strange. Is something wrong?" Mrs. B's hand on her shoulder shook Claire out of her trance.

"Oh, Mrs. B, Lucy's been hurt. She's in the hospital with a broken leg. And she can't go! The trip will have to be postponed, maybe even canceled. What am I going to do?"

That reminded her. "And poor Lucy. Her book! She needs her data checked before her deadline. What a mess!" Claire's words ended just short of a wail.

Mrs. B understood a crisis when she saw it and in less than five minutes she had issued instructions to the students working as clerks that day, grabbed her purse and ushered Claire out of the shop. In the cafe down the block she ordered tea for them both and a chicken salad sandwich to share while they discussed the situation.

It was the pragmatic Mrs. B who pointed out that it would be very costly to cancel the trip, and the people scheduled to go might prefer to continue without Lucy rather than give up the trip.

"But Lucy is the trip. She's the one who's been there before. She wrote the book, remember? All the rest of us are virgins, so to speak." They both smiled at Claire's apt description of the apprehensive yet eager group signed on for the *Untour.*

Lucy Springer had promised to transform this group into experienced world travelers during this one trip. They were all counting on that.

Mrs. B wouldn't agree. "She wrote the book for people like you to use. So if the book works you can do it without her. It would be great publicity."

"But she wrote the book for singles and couples traveling alone. This is a tour. It's not the same thing. Someone has to be in charge."

"Well, of course, dear. You would be in charge."

"Me, I've never been out of the States before. I can't be in charge." Claire realized her voice came out shriller than she meant it to be.

"My dear," Mrs. B patted her hand in that way she had, "you are a very in-charge lady. You'll handle it without a problem. Trust me. I've worked with you now for almost two years."

Claire looked at her with amazement.

Mrs. B nodded briskly. "Look at what you've done with the store. And your lecture series is now so popular people have to reserve seats."

Claire just continued to stare, her mouth open.

"Claire, dear, you've turned this shop into a thriving business. It's you, dear. You make it work."

"I thought it was all those hours of work, the sweat, the money, the concept that made it work." Claire answered dryly, not buying Mrs. B's theory.

Mrs. B laughed. "Anyone going into business does all that and look how many fail. You underrate yourself.

"And besides how difficult is it going to be? You know every step of the way. For heavens sake, I know every step of the way after listening to you and Lucy all these months. And the bus company is sending a guide, right? All the reservations are made. It's an *Untour*, remember? Everyone is grown up and responsible for his or her self. Just call them and ask. I bet you they'll want to go."

She saw the skepticism on Claire's face and bent forward. "I bet you one of those beautiful hand-knit sweaters from Yorkshire, like the one Lucy has, that I'm right."

Her smug expression was too much. Claire had to laugh. "So that's what you're after? You fraud. Okay! I will call everyone the minute we get back. And if I win you're going to have to go to some expensive specialty shop to get a sweater for me."

Mrs. B just nodded. She had no doubt who was getting that sweater.

* * *

"Hello?"

"Everything's a go. We're leaving Saturday as planned."

"You're sure?"

"Don't be ridiculous. It's all done. Just make sure you do your part. Once I step on that plane it's only a matter of time."

"Just make sure it's the right time. Everything hinges on that. You guaranteed me that."

"I told you, it's as good as done. You just see that you do your part." The connection broke abruptly.

Claire sighed with relief when her baggage was tagged and her boarding pass was firmly in her hand. She headed for the group of people crowded around Lucy's wheelchair, her one leg extended awkwardly, encased in a plastic and Velcro cast.

How did Lucy do it? Even with the practical nurse's assistance, Claire knew the effort to come to the airport must be exhausting her, but she wouldn't be dissuaded. She had to see them off. She said it was the least she could do now that she was shoving them from the nest without her careful supervision.

Claire counted off the people near Lucy then turned to check the ones still in line for check-in. Everyone was there. Thank goodness they were starting off without a hitch. She felt a clutch of panic. They were really going. And Lucy wasn't!

She had never in her wildest dreams expected she would be shepherding a group of novice travelers to England. Just one of the places she had never been. But she had always wanted to go there, and to Italy, and to a myriad of other destinations that seemed romantic and idyllic.

"Claire, can you stand over here next to Lucy?"

Claire squeezed in next to the wheelchair and laid her hand momentarily on Lucy's shoulder while different members of the group shot pictures of the ever changing group.

"How are you holding up?" she whispered.

Lucy nodded gamely, her mouth slightly pinched from the pain. "I think the pain pill is wearing off but it's almost time for you to board. I'm probably not going to wait until you take off."

"Of course not, you need to get home as soon as possible."

As the stragglers joined them Lucy said, "Okay everyone, do we have you all?"

Claire counted quickly, and then nodded.

"Well this is it, the big day. And in spite of all our careful planning we've had some last minute changes." She smiled wryly before continuing. "The most obvious is that I will not be with you as you've all been told. But Rosa Morino," she nodded towards the woman standing in the back, out of range of the lens on Tom's video camera, "has graciously consented to go in my place and verify the data I need to finalize my book. Some of you may have already met Rosa, my very able and talented editorial assistant. She's been with me for several months. Those of you who have not, please introduce yourselves at your earliest convenience."

Rosa nodded, visibly uncomfortable with the attention turned on her.

"Rosa had only one request. She has asked to be excluded from your photos. Her family doesn't do photographs and I promised her everyone would respect her wishes. So Tom, please do not include Rosa in your video." She smiled at the man who had his video camera extended from his eye since they had gathered together.

He removed the camera and smiled sheepishly, nodding his agreement at Rosa.

Lucy looked around the group until she got a nod of agreement from each person. "I know you'll all do what you can to assist Rosa, she's really been super about stepping in at the last moment to save my book deadline." She smiled with gratitude and the group murmured responses of appreciation.

Rosa seemed to shrink even further to the back of the group, out of range of the cameras still busily flashing and snapping as the tour members recorded their departure.

"Now, in addition, we have a new member of the group, Arnie White." She gestured to Arnie standing close to her chair. "Arnie hasn't had the advantage of attending our pre-trip meetings, so he isn't as up on every detail as the rest of you. I know you'll do your best to bring him up to speed and include him in the group. Again, take the time to get acquainted as soon as possible. I know Arnie will appreciate it."

Arnie nodded eagerly, smiling shyly.

"Of course, Claire will be with you and she is the person in charge. But remember the point of the Untour is to do things on your own whenever possible. When you arrive in London, Kingdom Coach Tours will have a representative to meet you and a guide from their offices will be accompanying you." She smiled encouragingly at all of them.

"All right, you'll all have to go through the scanner, the passport control and on to your gate. What is it?"

"Forty-two," came from the chorus of voices.

"Right, Gate 42. If anyone wants to change money before you get to England you can do it on the way to the gate. They should start boarding in about a half hour. You're all on your own until you meet the tour guide in Heathrow so remember all we talked about and don't forget to have fun!"

She waved gaily as the group moved off to the security gate.

Liz Cooley had been hovering over Lucy since she arrived, and now it was time to leave. "Don't worry Lucy. I'll make sure you get all the information you need."

She swooped down, scooped up the laptop case at Rosa's feet. "Come on, Rosa, I'm an old hand at this kind of thing," she said as she turned towards the security scanner. Rosa appeared stunned with surprise, but then her hand shot out and grabbed the computer case strap, jerking Liz to a stop so suddenly she almost fell over.

"That's my laptop and my job, thank you very much." The words barely made it through Rosa's angrily clenched jaw. She put the strap to the reclaimed laptop over her shoulder, picked up her tote bag and headed towards the gate.

Liz looked innocently at Claire and Lucy. "I was just trying to help."

Lucy shook her head gently. "I know you want to be helpful Liz but Rosa's right. It's her job and she's very capable of doing it. You just concentrate on having fun.

Leave the data collection to Rosa and the trip management to Claire. Okay?"

Liz nodded her agreement before heading for the gate. But her face was set with a look of stubborn determination, which didn't make them feel confident that she had gotten the message.

Lucy sighed, watching her retreating back. "Maybe you were right, Claire. Maybe I shouldn't have agreed to let her join the group. She is somewhat of an odd duck."

"Don't worry, Lucy. She'll be fine once we get there. I'm sure she's disappointed that you're not coming. You're her heroine. She just wants to make sure you get everything you need." They both watched her go through the security gate. "And it's only two weeks. How bad can it be?"

* * *

"Psst, Claire, are you awake?"

Snuggled into the blanket, suspended cozily in that zone between wakefulness and sleep, just as the plane was suspended between San Francisco and London, she ignored the whisper, pretending to sleep. She had more than enough of Liz already, and the trip had just started. Her stomach burned at the thought of the trip ahead. In spite of her cavalier assurance to Lucy, suspicion that Liz Cooley was going to be a constant problem gnawed at her. The little episode in the airport was the first indication. Then, as luck would have it, Liz and Rosa had seats side by side. That seemed to delight Liz and infuriate Rosa. Apparently the plane was so full that Rosa's appeal to the stewardess for a seat change had been futile.

Mrs. B had been right. Not one person had wanted to cancel or even postpone the trip, though they were all disappointed Lucy wouldn't be with them. No, they all wanted to go and worse, Lucy agreed with them. So now everyone but Lucy was on board, winging their way to adventure in merry old England.

Claire continued to be reluctant but Lucy reminded Claire that with her book deadline so near, someone had to verify her data. So it was decided Rosa, her invaluable administrative assistant, would travel in Lucy's place.

That solution didn't excite Claire. Rosa was apparently very good at what she did, which was research and editing, but she was a dour, remote individual. Somehow, when Claire had first heard of Rosa she had pictured her as a middle-aged southern rose, full-blown, soft-spoken and with graying blond hair. But Rosa had arrived tall and angular with dyed black hair and thick pancake makeup that threatened to crack from too much facial movement. Perhaps it was the reason she had never seen Rosa smile. Rosa wasn't like Katy, who had been with Lucy for several years. Katy had been funny and even saucy. Katy would have been a welcome addition to the tour group.

Poor Katy. She had been injured in a terrible car accident on Devil's Slide almost a year ago just after they first started talking about doing an Untour. Katy inadvertently delayed this trip once while Lucy dawdled with the book, waiting for her to get better. But after Katy had spent long months in the hospital and therapy, it became obvious that she might never be able to return to work. Lucy's publisher put an end to all the dissembling going on by forcing Lucy to commit to a completion date. And then he sent Rosa to help Lucy meet her commitment.

Rather than being angry, Lucy was grateful to have a publisher, who cared enough to do that. And Lucy was the first to sing Rosa's praises. She was apparently without peer in her field.

Now totally awake, Claire wanted to stretch, to roam the darkened aisles as she heard the sisters, Teri and Shar, doing. But she didn't dare. Liz was probably still awake and any movement on her part would be considered an invitation for company.

So she stayed still while her mind jumped from subject to subject.

Liz was the one mismatch in their group. Claire had noticed from the beginning but Lucy had defended her. Lucy had known Liz and her father for years.

It was a crime, Lucy explained, how Liz's selfish father had kept his daughter at his side, waiting on him, and helping him write his textbooks. He never had to share his success with her, nor pay her a wage. In fact, Lucy reported that she didn't ever remember him praising her, or acknowledging her contribution, as he would have had to do had she only been a hired employee. But Liz worshiped him and when he died, Liz, who was totally dependent on him for her life, was lost. Lucy saw this trip as a positive sign that Liz was trying to take charge of her life. But Claire speculated Liz was only attempting to replace her father with Lucy.

When Claire saw that Lucy wouldn't be dissuaded, she decided the group was big enough for her to avoid close contact with Liz for the two weeks. If Lucy didn't find Liz's hovering to be cloying, why would Claire care? But, of course, that was before she knew Lucy wouldn't be going and she would be in charge of the group instead of merely another member.

And now the obvious animosity between Rosa and Liz was surprising as well as distressing. Claire sighed. Maybe she should have offered to change seats with one of them, but already she felt she needed these few hours of peace. And, she decided, they were adults. They would be traveling together for two weeks; they would have to work it out.

Claire shifted trying to find a more comfortable position just as the sisters sailed down the aisle again. She watched them through slit eyes as they moved briskly forward. One was a little shorter and rounder than the other, and one used a strawberry hair rinse to the other's ash blonde. They told her people couldn't believe they were sisters until they got into their forties. Now, in their late fifties (perhaps even sixties), people thought they were twins. Their giggles and zest for life would add gusto to the group. They were encouragingly different than the Liz and Rosa combination. That thought made her feel better. It was a good group of people and they should be fun.

Claire noticed the cabin was now gray from the light seeping in around the window shades. She sneaked a look at her watch and then twisted it to the light to check it again. She must have slept. It was only three hours until landing.

Sudden excitement gripped her. I'm on my way to London Town, she realized. Somewhere, somehow she had forgotten that. After years of yearning for exotic destinations, she was finally doing it. She felt the smile reach her lips. It's not going to be so bad. After all, it's only two weeks.

* * *

Claire briskly pushed her cart of luggage past the customs officer following Mrs. Maus, who acted like she had done this a hundred times. She was still embarrassed about her original assumption that Mrs. Maus' age and her cane would hamper her ability to keep up with the rest of the group. Their first orientation meeting quickly disabused her of that notion. She realized the rest of the group would be lucky to keep up with the energetic senior.

"Joe, Joe, this way." Mrs. Maus pointed to a sign held high with "Springer Tour" written crudely on it.

Joe Onerato steered his cart across the traffic, not noticing the confusion he caused as people abruptly changed direction to avoid him, causing a domino effect of turbulence in the formerly fast flowing stream of luggage carts.

"Watch where you're going," he grumped at a teenager who veered her heavily loaded luggage cart so sharply to miss him that several of her cases flew off causing a pileup of carts behind her.

Joe shook his head at the teenager, unaware of his part in the mishap. "Kids today," he muttered as he joined the group. "Well, where is everyone? Let's get this show on the road."

The Mohney's, the Pederson's and the Sorini's, three couples from their group had already arrived. Mrs. Maus, Joe and Kim Whaley arrived just before Claire did. Looking behind her and seeing several more tour members coming towards them, she turned her attention to the woman holding the sign.

"I'm Claire Gulliver," she said and gesturing around her, "and this is the Springer Tour."

"Welcome to London." The smile was genuine and the accent charming. "I'm Emma Jones from Kingdom Coach Tours. I'll be your guide during your visit."

"Jones? We have a Jones on the tour."

Emma laughed. "Only one? Over here in any crowd there will probably be a couple of Jones'. In fact, almost the entire population of Wales is named Jones. You'll see when we get there."

She briefly consulted the papers in her hand before addressing Claire. "Now I have 23 people and 15 rooms. Is that correct? Has everyone come?"

Claire pulled her own list from the pocket on the side of her backpack and nodded. "Everyone was on the plane." She paused looking up as the group around them swelled. The sisters, Liz, the Martinez's, Arnie, Vern and Mike, and Annie Houghton reached them, chattering excitedly now that they were really in England.

"I guess the last few are still trying to get through the lines at passport control."

"Ladies and Gentlemen." It was surprising how Emma's voice carried through the din in the terminal. The tour group pressed closer, eager to hear what she had to say. "Welcome to England. Our coach is just outside waiting to take you on an orientation tour of London before we check into the hotel. Now while we're waiting for the rest of the group maybe those of you who have not had an opportunity to purchase English pounds would like to do so now at the booth across the way. I suggest you exchange enough for three days of expenses, and remember that for any sizable purchases you will get a better exchange rate by using your credit cards."

"What about the exchange rate? I thought exchange booths were notorious for gouging tourists."

Emma smiled at Joe, ignoring the grumpy sound of his comment. "Quite right! Of course, banks usually have the best rate, but even then you still need to shop around a bit. One bank's exchange rate and fees may not be the same as another bank's. However, the exchange booths in the terminals are offices of the local banks. On Tuesday we will be in Bath, and you will have a chance to exchange money again, perhaps at a better rate. In an emergency you can always exchange money at the hotels and you will find Exchange shops in every town."

Several people moved off towards the booths, while others repeated Emma's suggestion to the latecomers still straggling in. Claire watched Emma efficiently answer questions, direct more people to the money exchange booths, and then somehow herd them all out of the terminal to the waiting bus. And London!

"Why, it could be anywhere." The disappointment was clear as Alice said what everyone was thinking.

"Except we're going down the wrong side of the freeway," George Mohney muttered.

His wife's nose was pressed against the window. "For sure it's not California. Look how green the fields are." She added wistfully, "More like Michigan."

"Don't get impatient." Emma smiled. "You'll soon see some difference. I think this is a first tour for all of you, right? Well, after you've traveled a bit you'll notice the views between the major airports and the cities they service look about the same the world over. But we'll soon be in London, and as we won't check into the hotel until 1:00 we will spend some time giving you a tour of the city and getting you orientated for your few days here.

"Now, first thing for everyone to remember is always, always look both ways before stepping off the curb. You'd be surprised how many tourists we lose that way."

People smiled, relaxing, settling back as Emma started talking about the options they had as to how to spend their afternoon. She handed out packages of tickets, maps and information to be used during their few days in London. Some events were prepaid and the tickets were included, like the theatre on Sunday night, and the barge ride from Little Venice. But they each had to arrange to arrive at the appropriate places on their own. It was part of learning to travel. She quickly sorted out who wanted to do what and helped them organize into groups and plan their afternoon.

"Remember, taxis are cheap and will always take you where you want to go. But mass transportation is best if you want to really feel a part of London life."

"Once we get you checked into your hotel, you're on you own until Monday morning when I pick you up after breakfast. You have your itineraries and your set agenda items. When I see you Monday morning you'll be experienced travelers."

Claire looked around at the eager, apprehensive, and occasional scared expressions, feeling just like the rest of them but not daring to show it. She was their leader after all, and she needed to appear confident.

Suddenly, they were off the freeway, or as Emma called it, the motorway, and into streets lined with stone and brick buildings. Row houses lined the streets like San Francisco. Each house was attached to the other, with brightly painted doors leading to steps, which ended directly onto the sidewalks. Every little way a tree grew, and some steps had little pots of flowers squeezed into corners, but mostly it was just stone, brick and pavement. The bus was moving fast. It was hard to see it all. Emma's quick spiel seemed to tell them everything, point out everything.

The Thames was pronounced temms. Piccadilly Circus, which of course Claire knew wasn't, but still it was just a busy intersection. Leicester Square, but call it Lester or no one will know what you're talking about, was a teeming mass of people, restaurants and ticket booths. Buckingham Palace, the London Wall, the Tower Bridge seemed to fly by, then back the other side of the river with everyone crowding towards the windows to snap pictures across the river of the Houses of Parliament, Big Ben and Westminster Abbey. There was St. Paul's and the controversial Millennium Pedestrian Bridge. Across again, seeing the City, Dr. Johnson's House, Fleet Street, Downing Street. By the time they arrived at their hotel they were all dazed, glad to accept their keys and wander off to their rooms to sort out their luggage and thoughts.

* * *

Westminster Abbey London, England Day 3--Sunday Dear Mom, I went to church services here this morning and I can't begin to describe how awesome it was. I expected to see the queen coming down the aisle when they sounded the processional-- and the choir sounded like something we would pay money to hear at Davies Hall, if we were lucky enough to get the tickets. I'm having a great time. Lucy was right. We can and are doing it--and we're having fun. I have to rush now because I'm meeting the group at Little Venice and we're going on a barge down one of the canals. Every minute is an adventure. Tell Ruth that soon I'll be a world traveler in her league--I hope. Love, Claire	Mrs. Millicent Gulliver 124 13th Avenue San Francisco, CA 94119 USA AIR MAIL

* * *

"Here, Claire. We have room for you." Mary Pederson waved.

"I was afraid I'd miss the boat." Claire was a little out of breath from rushing. "I took the bus and misjudged how long it would take to get here." She moved through the crowded barge and sat where Mary indicated, nodding to others as she went past. "Did everyone have a good morning? I went to Westminster Abbey this morning. They were having a service so I just had to stay."

"We went over to the Speaker's corner in Hyde Park. It was great. John, you would have loved it. Anyone with a box to stand on gets up and talks. People stand around and listen, or argue with the speaker, or just walk away," Joan enthused. The Pederson's and the Sorini's were close friends and when John Pederson insisted he and his wife, Mary, take this trip instead of taking the kids somewhere, the Sorini's decided to come too.

"Uh, uh. Not if I had to get up to do it. I needed that time in bed." He glanced meaningfully at his wife. Mary blushed, a tiny smile hovering on her lips.

"John, you dog." Tom lifted his head from the eyepiece of his video camera and shook his head, an expression of admiration on his face.

"Leave them alone, Tom," his wife scolded him. "Not everyone feels the need to be up and out at the crack of dawn."

"What did you all do yesterday?" Claire tactfully changed the subject.

Mary smiled. "Glenda Martinez talked us into going to the Tea Dance at the Dorchester. You know they use to have one at the Hyatt Regency in San Francisco but I never went to it. This was truly elegant. They had an orchestra playing music from the 40's and 50's. And tuxedo clad waiters, with white gloves served the tea, and heaps of tiny sandwiches, and plates of pretty little cakes. They just kept bringing them so we just kept eating them. And then we danced and then we ate more. It was wonderful, wasn't it?"

Even the men agreed.

"It was so romantic and almost decadent. You know, all that culture out there to see and we're acting like we're in an old Cary Grant movie," Joan offered.

"Well, it was perfect. Glenda was right. It was just the way to start a trip to England. It kind of established a standard, you know?" Mary looked younger today, happy. Obviously she had stopped feeling guilty about leaving her kids behind.

"I'm so sorry Lucy couldn't come. This is going to be a great trip." Joan swept her hand around the packed barge, which was just angling out from its dock. "And, I notice everyone made the boat."

Arnie, sitting across the aisle, turned towards them. "Look this way so I can get your picture. Tom, just keep filming. That's perfect. Great!" Arnie smiled happily. "I'm so glad you let me join the tour, Claire. Really! This barge trip is great. I've never even heard of it before and I've listened to my friends talk about their trips for years." He looked around at the tour members scattered amongst the other passengers. "No wonder everyone made it. I, for one don't intend to miss any of the events Lucy suggested for us. Of course, I want to do some of the normal tourist things but this is what will make this trip."

"Yes, at the next cocktail party I'll say, "What? You've never taken the canal barge to Camden Market? My dear, you simply haven't seen London at all." Everyone laughed at Joan's droll voice.

Arnie turned back to the sisters, Terri and Shar, sitting on the other side of him, explaining what caused the laughter. Then the barge was moving down the narrow canal. They all felt a bit like voyeurs, peeking in the back windows of the rich and poor, the grand and crumbling buildings, the picturesque gardens of St. John's Woods and then into the Regency Park Zoo. They passed barges converted to homes, tied up at the banks, festooned with flowerpots, bicycles, and dogs. They could imagine themselves back in time when the canals moved the major goods throughout England. They became immersed in a time when whole families lived, worked, and died on the barges they carted goods on. And, far too soon, they disembarked before the barge moved into the complicated Camden Locks.

Claire stood there to watch the barges, trapped in place while the bargemen raised and lowered the waters to move them to the next section of canal. Claire was fascinated by the skill and apparent ease the men demonstrated to complete what must be backbreaking labor. When she finally turned back to the bustling street market she saw most of their tour group had been swallowed in the crowd.

"Hey, Rosa. How's it going for you?" Claire caught up with her, feeling a little guilty for not checking with her earlier.

"I've confirmed most of the data I needed yesterday afternoon so I thought I'd join the group on this trip." Rosa sounded a little defensive.

"Well, of course, Lucy means you to participate. After all, that's what she would do and you're her stand in. I just wanted to see if you needed some help. If you do, I hope you'll let me know."

Rosa made a grimace as she jerked her head toward Liz, who Claire saw was headed their way. "Don't worry. I have more help than I'll ever need. She's driving me crazy."

"Oh, Rosa, still?" Claire gave Rosa an empathic nod and murmured, "I'll try." She turned as Liz joined them.

"Oh, Liz. Good! I need some help and you're just the person." She took Liz's arm firmly turning her toward the packed streets, ignoring her struggle to resist, confiding warmly, "Lucy told me about a place out here that makes wonderful sofa pillows out of antique rugs and draperies. I think I need to look at them for the reading alcove at the shop. What do you think?"

She managed to keep the reluctant Liz with her until they found and selected four attractive pillows. But while Claire was making arrangements to have her purchases shipped, Liz escaped. Actually, Claire wasn't inclined to look for her. She thought the chances of Liz finding Rosa in the ever-changing thong of vendors and shoppers was as remote as her chance to find Liz. And she didn't intend to ruin her day by spending it with Liz.

She had done her duty and now she was free to wander at will. It was an eclectic crowd, snatches of conversations in various languages drifted around her. Even the words she understood had a different sound, making the market seem just that much more exotic.

Couples with arms about each other debated where to lunch. Families were trying to keep track of their children, young teenagers were darting in packs, giggling and flirting with each other. The older youths glided like panthers, cigarettes dangling from tight lips, with orange, purple, and green hairstyles. Tattoos vied with rings piercing a variety of body parts that made Claire shudder to see, while their eyes darted slyly to make sure everyone noticed how cool they were.

Claire paused over a display of brass lapel pins offered by a young artist. The artist used old greeting card motifs that he cast in brass and the results were so unique she couldn't choose a favorite, ending up by buying three before tearing herself away. And she couldn't resist trying a hot meat pie. She strolled on nibbling at the flaky crust, careful not to lose a crumb. She caught up to Kim Whaley and Annie Houghton sorting through vintage clothes in a crowded stall. She gladly joined them and when they left, each of the three had a naval uniform jacket affixed with gold braid and brass buttons they were delighted with. And the price was a steal.

Arnie White and Betty Brown caught up with them as they headed towards the Tube Station. They compared purchases and lunches, already speculating about the evening ahead.

"Oh, oh, this doesn't look good." Kim said what they were all thinking.

They came to halt in front of Rosa, a thunderous expression on her face as she glared at Liz, whose righteous look, as everyone was already learning, meant trouble. Warren was trying to placate Rosa, his face red with effort. But Claire could see it wasn't working.

"I don't want my picture taken. Liz knows that. I've explained it before. It is part of my religion. She did it on purpose. She obviously doesn't respect my beliefs. I want the film."

"Don't be ridiculous. I have all kinds of pictures on this film. I'm not going to throw away a record of the trip just because you think I took your picture. I told you I didn't even see you. I was taking a picture of the street scene. You're probably not even in it."

Rosa shook her head. "I saw you sneaking up on me. I want that film."

"Liz," Claire said with exasperation. "You know how Rosa feels. She explained it to all of us. We all agreed to respect her wishes. How could you?"

"I didn't. I was taking a picture of the street and I swung my camera around trying to get just the right composition. I didn't even see Rosa and her boyfriend until after I snapped the picture. I don't think she's even in it."

Liz didn't want to budge but, seeing Claire's expression and then looking at the rest of the group, she sighed and gave in.

"All right. All right. I don't think I got her but when I get them developed if she is in the picture, I'll destroy it and the negative, no matter how good the picture is. Okay? Will that satisfy everyone?"

It clearly didn't satisfy Rosa but, with everyone approving the compromise, she grudgingly agreed. Arnie and Warren moved off with Rosa, leaving Liz to join the others.

"So, what boyfriend?" Claire heard Betty ask Liz.

"Never saw him before but it certainly looked as if they knew each other. As soon as she saw me she said something and he just disappeared into the crowd."

"Well, who would have thought it of Rosa," Annie said to Kim. "You and I were all dolled up last night looking for romance and Rosa finds it in a street market. We better keep an eye on her. We might get some tips."

"Come on ladies. I'm sure it was just a harmless encounter." Claire interjected commonsense into the conversation. "Rosa's never even been to England before. If it was someone she knew she'd be so surprised at the coincidence she'd be telling us all about it."

That made so much sense they didn't pursue the issue. When Betty reminded them of the time, the incident was forgotten. They still had to get ready for the evening's activities.

CHAPTER THREE

"All right, Fenster. What's going on? I was scheduled to tee off at noon, so this better be good."

Fenster nodded. His boss was an avid golfer and this assignment in London, the last in a long illustrious career, seemed to be his preparation for retirement in Florida. But even though he was currently a short-timer, Fenster knew better than to regard him as less than the professional he was.

"I'm sorry but I felt you needed to hear about this one, sir. The Brits picked up some hints that something big was coming down. They have been working on it, but were unable to pin anything down until this showed up."

He put a facsimile of the brochure for the Lucy Springer Untour on the desk.

Fenster waited, suppressing his impatience while his boss scrutinized the brochure as if he was considering signing on. It was this attention to detail that had made him so successful over the course of his career.

When Fenster saw Horace Ames was nearing the end, he slipped the list of tour members on the immaculate desk.

"This is a very preliminary list of the tour group. We have our people in the States working on full background checks but so far they appear to be a pretty mundane group of Americans. Just about what you'd expect." He stopped abruptly, swallowing uneasily under Ames' piercing look.

"If this is such a mundane group, why are we even interested?"

Horace Ames was sharp. And tough. Everyone agreed there. It was hard keeping up with him, say nothing about being ahead of him. And to add to the difficultly of working with him was the name thing. It was hardly appropriate to call him Ames, as they referred to him amongst themselves, and Horace was unthinkable. Fenster often wondered what kind of parent would name a baby Horace? And what Ames would have been like if he had been named Bob or Dave or Scott? He took the safe road whenever he had to deal with him directly, using his military background as an excuse to call him *sir*, even though his seniority and long relationship with Ames probably meant he could have gotten away with calling him by his first name.

"Of course, of course. Someone, somewhere has some interest in them and so perhaps they are not what they appear to be."

Fenster watched Ames scan the list, then say, "Okay, tell me what we know about each of them."

Fenster started with Lucy Springer, explaining she was a well-known and nationally recognized author of travel books. She frequently lectured and even, on occasion, appeared on TV talk shows. But as it turned out, she wasn't even with the group. That seemed suspicious but proved to be nothing more than an accident. There was no doubt that her leg was broken. He had a copy of the X-ray. Lucy, herself, turned out to be their main source of information about the other tour members. They interviewed her extensively under the guise of writing publicity about the tour for her publisher.

Claire Gulliver played a key role in the tour and was known personally to Lucy, and as it turned out, she was also well-known to the San Francisco Police Department. It seems her father had been one of their own. He was a police sergeant, but was killed in the line of duty when she was six. She was raised conservatively by a cautious mother, understandable given her experience in life. A few years back Claire had somehow gotten involved in a major drug deal when she did a favor for one of her mother's friends. Not only had she been resourceful enough to escape with her life, but ultimately, she had been instrumental in assisting the police crack the case. The police captain recounted the story with as much pride as if she had been his own kid, albeit well past the kid age. She had been the neighborhood librarian until, after her involvement in the drug deal, she had moved to the Peninsula and opened Gulliver's Travels Bookshop. Nothing seemed very sinister there.

Glenda and Alex Martinez have been married forty years and never been out of the country unless you count their one trip to Victoria. Alex works for a large insurance agency and is planning to retire soon. Glenda is a full-time grandmother and a part-time bookkeeper for a large real estate broker.

Mrs. Maureen Maus is a spry seventy-eight. She first nursed her mother, then her ailing husband. He died last year leaving her with lots of time and no responsibilities.

She volunteers at the Senior Center, serving lunches to those seniors younger in years but older in expectations.

Liz Cooley has never been married. She is somewhere in her fifties—it was hard to obtain information about her. Many people knew her father, who she assisted until his death a couple of years ago, but no one knew anything about her, describing instead her father and his accomplishments.

Fenster hadn't yet obtained her exact birth date, but he would get it from her passport records shortly. According to his notes, Liz looks, and apparently acts, like a character out of a Victorian novel.

Mrs. Teresa (Teri) Bouten and Mrs. Sharon (Shar) Waldoe are sisters, Teri widowed and Shar divorced. Lucy said they were in their fifties, but their driving records disclosed their ages to be ten years older. Lying about their ages is hardly criminal. They grew up in a large, close family in Southern California but spent their adult lives five hundred miles apart. Now that their families have grown and become independent, they have grown closer to each other again. This is the first trip they're taking together.

Annie Houghton is a paralegal for a fast growing computer software company. The money is great, the work exciting but the backlog of contracts to produce and approve is overwhelming. It's difficult to take time for a vacation. But Annie needs it and she has accumulated so much vacation time the Human Resources Department at her company has warned her she may lose it if she doesn't take it. She isn't about to let that happen. This tour was the answer.

Kim Whaley is in her late twenties and has limited time and money but her friend, Annie Houghton, talked her into using a small inheritance she received to finance this trip.

Fenster had little suspicion of either of these girls. Their pasts were very easy to piece together.

Vern Higbee teaches literature at the State University. He is in his late forties, a natty dresser, very conservative, perhaps even prudish, and he is gay. He never came out of the closet, as he has been very open about his preferences. When he realized he was different than others in his Midwest home he moved to San Francisco where he fit in comfortably. He and Mike Joseph have been a devoted couple for over fifteen years and their decision to move to the Peninsula, just before the AIDS epidemic reached full swing, was fortunate.

Mike Joseph is a CPA in the San Francisco Offices of a major accounting firm. He looks twenty years younger than Vern but isn't. He attributes his youthfulness to his workout schedule and Vern's cooking. They have wanted to travel overseas but somehow never got around to it. So when Lucy Springer announced she would be taking a group with her to finalize her next book, he and Vern were the first to sign up.

Alice Jones is in her forties. She's been divorced for ten years and is a close friend of Vern and Mike, since she was their neighbor when they all lived in the city. She works in a major California Bank and has somehow survived the reorganizations and downsizings that have been going on for the last several years. Lucy reported that Alice decided life was too uncertain to wait for retirement to travel. She was going to do it now and every chance she got.

John and Mary Pederson are in their thirties. John insisted on this trip, while Mary wanted a family trip to Hawaii. John was quoted as saying that for eleven years they have always taken the kids. It's time to treat themselves to adult entertainment. His wife reluctantly agreed. After all, John worked so hard to finally make manager of one of the huge local supermarkets, she felt he deserved this trip. The children are staying with John's parents so there is really nothing to worry about. But Mary feels guilty about leaving them.

Tom and Joan Sorini are friends of the Pederson's and have vacationed on Shasta Lake with them several times. This trip sounded so great they decided to come too. Joan has no qualms about leaving her kids with her sister, because she watched her sister's kids last year. She's vocal about her joy of getting some time, alone, with Tom. Tom is a video freak and is determined to record the entire trip for his friends and family to experience with them.

Joe Onerato is a crusty, old Italian who lives alone and spends most of his days playing cards at the Senior Center in North Beach or playing bocce ball in the park. He retired and turned his family business over to his son after his wife died ten years ago. Joe's son is worried about him. He thinks he's bored but doesn't know it and won't take any suggestions. His son signed him up for the trip as a surprise. Joe didn't have the energy for the battle that would ensue if he canceled, so he's going. But he doesn't want to, and he insisted on his own room. He wasn't sleeping with strangers.

Warren Grey went through a very painful divorce and hasn't seemed interested in developing any social relationships since then. He's a tall, thin shy man, but his shyness only seems to attract the women. He concentrates on his work, his running schedule and his son. His son usually spends summers with his father but this year he is only coming for a week. This has upset Warren and this trip is his way to start to redirect some of his energy. He realizes with his son growing, he needs to have his own space to do things with his friends. Warren doesn't want their time together to be a burden to him.

Betty Brown is thirtyish, attractive and remote. She won't share her room. Her clothes, style and manner identify her as an up-and-coming executive. She is pleasant but the smile doesn't reach her eyes. She volunteers nothing about herself. However, Fenster knows it won't take long to solve that mystery; his agents were gathering information even now.

George and Florence Mohney have been retired about seven years. George was a chemist at a large pharmaceutical company. They spend their summers in Michigan, where they raised their children. Then they spend part of the year visiting their daughter in Montana and the rest of their time in the retirement community near their son and his family in California. Their son and daughter-in-law attended Lucy's lecture at Gulliver's and talked their in-laws into joining the group.

Rosa Morino is Lucy Springer's assistant. Rosa has only been with Lucy for six months. Dour and silent most of the time, she is apparently known for her efficiency. Her publisher recommended Rosa to Lucy. When Lucy broke her leg, Rosa, like the professional she is, agreed to take Lucy's place on the tour to verify all the data in her book. Who better? Rosa had done most of the arrangements, and she knew the book, having entered the first draft into the computer. She was taking the laptop with her to make the adjustments needed for prices, addresses and resources.

Fenster finished with, "Arnold 'Arnie' White looks like a computer nerd and he probably is. But his joining the tour at the last minute makes him suspect, and so far we haven't turned up much on him. However, we'll know everything about him before long."

Fenster paused, having come to the end of the list, racking his brain for any detail he overlooked.

"So what else is there? Something besides all this got you excited enough to bring me in on Saturday." Ames was still irritated about missing his tee off time.

Fenster nodded. "That last transmission they picked up was pretty garbled but there were a few words that got our attention. One was the second reference to this tour." He gestured toward the brochure. "The other...." He paused, deliberately adding drama. "The other was Guiness."

Ames' face didn't change but his eyes did, and his ears were getting red, a singular trait of his, indicating his blood pressure was rising.

"Guiness?" The word exploded from him. "Guiness? Who's on this? Why didn't you tell me that first?"

He stood up abruptly, a look of cunning on his face. "This could be it. We might finally get that bastard. I want to be kept informed, any day, anytime. If one of them burps, it better be in a report to me. Don't let anyone screw this one up, Fenster." He slammed his hand on the desk.

Fenster nodded. "Don't worry we will be with this group every inch of the way. This will be a close collaboration with our friends here. They want him as badly as we do, perhaps more so. Actually, if they hadn't identified that tour as American we'd still be in the dark. If there is anything to this we're going to get him," he growled with determination. Then at Ames' nod of dismissal he headed for the door, glad to be through with this part of it, already thinking about the problem of keeping an entire tour group under surveillance.

* * *

Claire let herself out into the hall, still a little groggy from sleep but anxious to assuage her hunger with a whopping English style breakfast. She headed down the corridor and through the door to the next hall, thinking about that same old nightmare. Fortunately the alarm rescued her before she got to the part where she usually started screaming. For that she was grateful. Why was it that the familiarity of the dream never reduced its terror?

Then when she dragged herself out of bed she confronted a real nightmare in the bathroom mirror. The wrinkles at the corner of her eyes had somehow multiplied overnight and that slight line across her brow was now definitely a crease. She tried to blame the sallow color of her skin on the low wattage light bulb, but she couldn't quite convince herself of it.

Claire came up short, facing the end of the corridor. She looked around, sure she hadn't been this way before, not clear on how she got here. This hotel was extremely confusing. The floors didn't seem to be on the same level in each section and each section was connected to the others by doors, steps and odd corridors.

She chose the door directly in front of her and was relieved to see it contained a set of stairs. She wasn't always sure she was headed in the right direction, but the one thing she knew was she needed to go down to reach the dining room. She stepped out onto the landing. The impact took her breath away even as the momentum spun her around. Then unable to stop herself she was down, fortunately partially cushioned by some of the bags that seemed to be flying everywhere.

She lay there a moment, gasping for air, then tried to lever herself up on her elbow.

The groan came from beneath her and she was suddenly aware that besides the sharp corners of luggage there seemed to be a person under her that her elbow was digging into.

"Watch it!" The sharp directive was followed by a string of murmured comments of which Claire caught only a few words, oaf, bloody cow and worse.

"Oh, I'm so sorry. Just a minute and let me get up." She looked for a handhold and finally latched onto one of the supports, pulling her off the heap but pushing another of the cases down the stairs. She was acutely aware that her knee apparently had caused some damage as she rose to her feet, at least judging by the moan that came from the man she could now see under what was left of the luggage.

She bent over him, offering her hand. "Are you hurt? Can I help you up?"

He glared at her. "Not bloody likely. You've done enough damage."

She withdrew her hand, affronted. He was very rude. And he had run into her. He knocked her down and so far he hadn't even said he was sorry or asked if she was hurt.

She drew herself up and looked at him. He was not young, with sandy hair, probably from going gray. His skin was weathered as if he was outdoors a lot. He looked fit, wiry even or maybe she would describe him as whippy, but that was because of his attitude. When he finally stood up she saw he was only a few inches taller than her average height, so for a man that wasn't very tall. All and all, she wasn't impressed, especially with his manners.

"Well, I can at least help you gather up the luggage." She looked around, hoping it was packed well or there would be some breakage, especially in the case that was halfway down the stairs.

"No thank you! I think it would be best if you took yourself out of the service stairwell and off to wherever it is that you belong." The sarcasm dripped heavily from his words.

Claire's cheeks burned with anger. "I would be happy to do that if I knew how to get there." Her voice was haughty now. After all, she only wanted her breakfast.

He opened the door and pointed to another door along the corridor. Claire left feeling very much like a chastised child. She was still fuming, testing for bruises that were sure to pop up from her encounter, as she entered the dining room.

"Claire, good morning." Teri, the sister with the strawberry hair, moved her oversized purse out of the way inviting Claire to sit beside her.

Shar, the blonde was bubbling, "Wasn't that a great play? That theatre is so picturesque. And somehow a Noel Coward play was so..., well, so English."

"It was all right, if you like old English movies. Frankly I liked that place we went afterwards." George Mohney looked like a person who loved his beer.

Claire gave the waitress her order and then Vern, who just sat down, ordered for both he and Mike.

“Where is Mike this morning?” Teri asked. “Oh, there he is. Mike. Mike!” She waved at him as he paused at the door.

Mike was very popular with the other members of the tour. His outrageous personality made them all laugh.

“I ordered for you.”

Mike nodded as he sat down between Vern and Florence Mohney, unfolding his napkin. “I was talking to Joe.”

“Joe? He never talks.” George looked up amazed. “Just grouches.”

Mike laughed. “Not so grouchy this morning. He’d been out with Mrs. Maus.” He looked about the table, a glint in his eye. “I think that the grouch’s days are numbered.” He paused to build suspense. “I think Mrs. Maus will straighten out our Joe before we get home. Anybody want to bet with me?”

Mrs. Maus, no one even attempted to call her Maureen, was up and out for a brisk walk each morning. Several others followed her lead, cramming their days with more activities than Claire thought was possible.

Teri and Shar nodded.

“He did come with us this morning, but he complained most of the way,” Teri reported.

“Teri, he wasn’t so bad. He’s probably just lonely.” Shar gently reproached her sister. Then trying to explain further, “He was so attached to his wife, he’s just lost without her.”

Teri didn’t agree. “He’s been a widower for ten years. He’s just a grouch and everyone has let him be one. But not Mrs. Maus. You wait. She’ll get him to break that habit.”

The waitress returned with tea and coffee, then again with the breakfast. Claire warily contemplated the boiled egg perching in an hourglass shaped cup.

"Can I help?" Vern reached over and deftly sliced off the top with his knife. "There. Put a little salt and pepper in there and use this little spoon to just eat right out of the shell."

"How did you do that? I finally ended up peeling mine," Shar said, astonished.

"You should have ordered the traditional breakfast like we did," George said.

But Shar just shook her head. "It was fried everything, including the bread and some revolting black thing called blood sausage. Ugh, no, thanks! But next time I'll wait for Vern to crack open my soft-boiled eggs."

"We had an English woman as a housekeeper when I was growing up. And she made wonderful soft-boiled eggs. Perfect. So, of course, we all had to learn how to eat them properly." Vern smiled. "I was very fond of her. I used to follow her around like a puppy. My parents were so busy all the time but she always had time for me."

He glanced at Claire, who had just finished her egg. "I think you'll find another under the bottom of your cup."

Claire retrieved the second egg and attempted to slice off the top as neatly as Vern had done the first. She laughed with the rest as she fished out the bits of shell before dipping her spoon in to pierce the yolk.

The flash caught her with the spoon full of egg on its way to her mouth, startling her enough to cause the spoon, egg and all, to end up her nose. She grabbed her napkin dabbing blindly, blinking furiously, trying to clear the spots from her vision.

"Liz, don't do that!" Vern snapped. "Really, show a little consideration by warning us before you take a picture. It would be nice to give us a chance to compose ourselves or even smile."

"But I don't want posed pictures. I want the pictures to be spontaneous. It's much better to have them *au naturale.* You'll see when I get them developed.

"Besides, I'm doing this for Lucy. She might want to use some to promote her book," Liz tossed out righteously as she moved on in search of her next target.

"We need Mrs. Maus to adopt her," Mike muttered. The others added comments and complaints.

Claire just wasn't in the mood for Liz this morning, either in person or as a subject of conversation. So instead she concentrated on eating while the conversation flowed around her. Finally, her breakfast finished and her vision cleared, she pushed back from the table. "Well, I'd better move if I'm going to be ready for our *prompt* departure."

"The bus is here. I saw them stowing some of the bags," George said checking his watch and nodding at his wife.

"Coach," reminded Shar. "Remember Emma said they call them coaches," she explained as she and Teri prepared to leave the table.

CHAPTER FOUR

Claire thought it ironic that she actually found her way back to her room through the jumble of corridors without a hitch. Somehow that success restored her confidence. After all, she was the leader and she felt she could cope with anything. So after gathering up her odds and ends, she paused only long enough to examine her face for traces of egg yolk. This time, studying the mirror, she was kinder to herself. It still surprised her that while she was always considered rather plain she had somehow grown into her looks so that now, middle-aged, she was considered attractive. Not beautiful, of course, as she studied her face critically, but even she admitted that she looked interesting. The wrinkles were still there. That was a blow because she always considered her fine textured skin to be her best feature and now it was going. But her hair was okay. The strands of gray blended with the light brown and looked like she had an expensive highlight job, which her expensive cut showed to its best advantage. And her figure was good; she was lean, strong and had curves in the right places. And she couldn't complain that she didn't look like those middle-aged movie stars, because she had never resembled them when she was young and she had no expectations of looking like them now. After all she was in her descending years; she had turned forty last year. So what could she expect? She was what she was.

She slipped her backpack over her shoulder and picked up her tote bag, taking one last look around to make sure she had everything. She found her way downstairs without further mishap wondering how she had gotten so confused every time before. She saw that Rosa was checking the final bills with the hotel manager so she proceeded to the bus to confirm today's schedule with Emma, their Kingdom Coach Tour representative.

"Good morning Claire." Mrs. Maus was already settled halfway down the aisle of the huge bus. "Look how much room we have. Harold had to bring a bigger bus, the one we used before was only for city tours. This one has a galley and restroom, just like the airplane. Isn't this grand?"

Claire nodded agreement as she looked around. The bus seemed way too big for their group, but Emma had told her that the addition of Arnie to their group had caused the tour company to assign them a bigger coach. The company was very strict about adhering to the rules about the maximum number of passengers allowed on each vehicle.

She apologized. It was the result of her inexperience. She hadn't even thought about the local transportation when she agreed to let Arnie come. She had been so pleased Warren was willing to share a room with Arnie so they didn't have to book another room at every stop. She just assumed that was all that mattered.

"Have you seen Emma this morning?" she asked Mrs. Maus, looking around for their guide.

"Oh, didn't you know? Emma isn't with us. Her mother was taken sick, suddenly, so of course she had to go home."

Claire's stomach clenched with dismay as she realized how much she was relying on Emma. "Oh, no, not another casualty?"

"Don't worry, dear." Mrs. Maus said calmly. "They sent us the most delightful young man. His name is Jack and he's very good. I can tell already."

Claire smiled uneasily, not convinced. She turned to hurry back down the aisle only to crash, nose to nose with the same sandy-haired, whippy man from the stairwell, who had apparently come up the aisle behind her.

Claire, blinking rapidly to clear the bright lights flashing in the momentary blackness, gently touched her nose to make sure it wasn't broken.

"Oh, my dear, are you all right? Do you need to sit down? Can I get you a wet cloth?" Mrs. Maus was very concerned.

Claire shook her head, managing a tight smile while she attempted to regain her composure.

Mrs. Maus did the honors. "Claire, this is Jack. Jack, here's Claire Gulliver. She's in charge of our tour, as I'm sure you already know from Emma." Mrs. Maus graciously introduced them.

"Of Kingdom Coach Tours." He backed up a step, distorting his face to stretch his nose, his hand creeping up to touch it tentatively. "We really need to stop meeting this way, Luv."

Claire was annoyed. Actually she was very close to angry. She didn't like the way he acted, as if he was laughing at her. And she didn't like that twice in one morning they had collided. And her nose hurt. Why was he always where he shouldn't be?

And he wasn't a young man!

But then she conceded perhaps he would seem so to Mrs. Maus.

"I'm very sorry to hear about Emma." She grudgingly held out her hand for his firm grip. "I understand you're taking her place? I believe we need to discuss today's schedule." She started down the aisle, forcing him to retreat, saying firmly, "Not here. Outside, please!"

She squeezed past him and down the steps just as Arnie approached. She paused at the surprise on his face when he saw Jack.

"Arnie White, Jack—," Claire began.

"Hanford, of Kingdom Coach Tours." Jack stuck out his hand as he stepped out of the bus.

"Yes, our guide. Emma was called away." She looked at Arnie closely. "Do you know each other?"

Arnie blushed, stammering, "No, but Jack looks so much like a guy I work with I got confused about where I was. Nice to meet you, Jack."

"Well, they say everyone has a twin," Jack quipped to Claire as she led him to one side, out of the path of the people trying to get on the bus.

"Mr. Hanford how much do you know about our tour? I'm afraid I'm very disappointed about Emma. I was really relying on her knowledge to get us through the trip. Our tour leader broke her leg last week and had to cancel. So we're all novices."

"Don't worry, Luv. I have Emma's crib notes and I've always been keen on history. I think I can cover most of the questions and perhaps even make a contribution."

"Well, let's go over the schedule for today."

"Ah, a bit of a test?"

Claire's annoyance flared again only to be forgotten when she saw Rosa struggling with her tote, the computer, a portable file box and a large suitcase while the wind tore at the clutch of papers in her left hand.

Claire captured the papers to Rosa's relief. "This is Jack Hanford, Rosa. He's our new guide. Emma's mom took ill."

Rosa handed over the suitcase and file box with only a headshake at Jack's attempt to take the laptop. "Good morning. No, not the laptop. I'll need it on the bus."

She explained to Claire, as close to flustered as she seemed to get, "I got so busy this morning with the notes from yesterday that I didn't get my bag out in time for pick-up. I was afraid I was going to miss the bus, I mean, coach."

She was so conscientious, so serious, completely devoid of humor.

Claire told her earnestly, "Rosa, look, you don't have to work all the time. Lucy wanted you to enjoy yourself, too."

"That's nice of you, Claire, but I have to get it all down. You know Lucy needs this information. I'm sure it won't be like this every day. Now that we're heading out into the country, I won't have so many sources to check each day." She nodded her head towards Liz, now climbing onto the bus, her camera at ready in her hand. "Besides, if I become lax you know who is poised to take over."

Claire nodded. "I know she's been making a nuisance of herself. She just isn't very good with people. You know she spent her whole life with her father, managing his affairs, doing his research and now that he's gone she seems to be lost. I'll talk to her again."

"Well, as long as she stays away from me I don't care what she does." Rosa boarded the bus ahead of Claire, taking a seat in the back, a long way from where Liz sat.

Betty Brown was the last one on the bus. As usual she arrived impeccably dressed and coiffured, looking stunning. Claire noted Jack's obvious approval of Betty as he gallantly assisted her up the steps of the bus, wondering sourly if he was going to prove to be a ladies' man. That thought gave her a start.

Ladies' man? Where did that come from? She was starting to think like one of her mother's friends. No, she wouldn't let herself be like that. Everyone was an adult on this trip. She didn't need to supervise anyone's behavior. And, she decided firmly, she wouldn't!

Jack stood and counted heads. Then, giving a signal to Harold, the doors closed and the coach pulled out into the traffic.

"Good day to you. I'm Jack. Your 'man' for the trip, and if you notice I'm not as dainty and eye appealing as Emma is when serving tea. I'm sure you'll appreciate my brawn when it comes time to heft those bags you're so attached to." His grin was wolfish but Claire could see the others responding to his style.

"Kingdom Coach Tours is pleased to have this opportunity to show you our country. And my job is to make sure you enjoy yourselves.

"Now, we have this great coach with a galley and our own loo so we are fairly self-sufficient."

Jack paused, seeing the confusion. "Oops, I see we have hit a language barrier already. Loo is the common word for toilet. I'm sure that bit of information will come in handy for some of you." He waited patiently for the laughter to die down. "And Kingdom has assigned their best driver, Harold, here, to make sure we travel safely."

Harold intent on maneuvering through the London streets grinned in the mirror and waved his hand.

"So sit back and relax. We'll arrive at Stonehenge in about two hours and then on to Avebury for lunch. We should be arriving at Hilliary Hall in time for tea. Don't forget to review your information packet and if you have any questions I'll try to answer them."

Jack cocked an eyebrow at Claire but she buried her nose in the information packet, not willing yet to like him, or to forgive him for his rudeness this morning.

* * *

The time on the road passed pleasantly enough. Mike arranged an afternoon tennis tournament with Kim, Annie and Tom after Jack told him that the Hilliary Hall courts were excellent and the hotel could supply them all with rackets. Vern and Joan were joining Mrs. Maus' entourage to explore the grounds and adjoining town of Castle Combe before tea. Rosa wasn't committing herself and Liz was frustrated, wanting to shadow Rosa but afraid she would miss something with one of the other groups. Warren, Alex Martinez and Arnie were talking about a round of golf, if they could get on the course.

The rest were still thinking about their options when the first view of a hilltop with stones appeared on the right side of the bus. Everyone crowded to that side, pressing cameras to the windows in spite of Jack's assurances that they would have lots of picture opportunities.

They scrambled off the bus into the bleakness of the big barren parking lot. The wind tore around them.

"Pretty grim, isn't it?" Arnie fell into step with Claire as they trudged toward the site, staying on the path as the signs directed them, following the never ending string of tourists.

"Well, Arnie, this looks like your kind of weather. Not a bathing suit in sight." She was disappointed. Their first stop, and it was appallingly commercial. Her eyes were weeping from the wind as she struggled to fasten her jacket more securely. She wiped her eyes, set her sunglasses more firmly in place for protection from the wind and then looked up to see where she was going. She came to an abrupt halt. The giant stones dwarfed her, robbing her of speech. All she had read, all the pictures she had seen had misled her. She had not been ready for Stonehenge.

The size and number of the stones was amazing. How could they even be called stones? The starkness of the terrain, heightened by the howling wind and the gray sky, raised goose bumps on her scalp. She forgot the group. She didn't see the other tourists milling about, aiming cameras at every angle. She walked away from Arnie without a thought, totally caught up in this giant monument.

It was a message from the past. Someone had the imagination, the power, and the tenaciousness to move these mountainous stones to this lonely hilltop. Then, out of whimsy, or for a mysterious purpose, had stacked them like building blocks.

Why? Who? When?

* * *

Liz came for her, urging her to hurry. Everyone was waiting, she said. But Claire returned at her own pace, coming back to her world slowly, no longer worried about this trip or its minor problems. She now knew why people needed to travel, to experience things that couldn't be imagined, that were beyond description. Pictures and words could never convey the mystery, the grandeur, the awe created by these stones on this hill.

"Feeling a little fey?" Jack asked with a lift of the eyebrow.

Claire laughed, surprised at his perception. "How did you know?"

"You have the look. It affects some people that way. For others, they're just big stones." He nodded towards the rest of the tour members straggling into the coach.

By the time the bus arrived at Avebury, Claire was hungry and a little embarrassed at the thought she might have been rude to Arnie. She made a point to seek him out and was grateful to find he apparently hadn't noticed her earlier desertion. The Avebury stones were interesting but, for her, they lacked the drama of Stonehenge. She was happy to buy a sandwich and drink and follow Mrs. Maus' group around the inner circles of stones and through the village before breaking off to explore the small museum. There she couldn't resist buying a book titled, *Stonehenge, Myths, Legends, Facts*. Already, she planned to find a quiet time to relax with a cup of tea and learn more about those stones and the people who moved them.

The trip from Avebury to Hilliary Hall was peaceful. Many of the group took the time to snooze but Claire couldn't sleep. The coach was lumbering down tiny roads, past cottages and minute villages. Glimpses of farms, cottages and large Manor houses occasionally appeared tantalizingly through the trees. Glenda Martinez slipped into the seat beside her and they chatted quietly about what they were seeing.

"Lucy told me that this is one of her favorite places in all of England," Claire told her. And you know we're going mostly to her favorite places."

"Really? What's so special about Hilliary Hall?" Glenda wanted to know.

"I guess because it was an old manor house that's been converted to a hotel but still feels like it's someone's house. And this little village is supposed to be one of the prettiest in the Cotswold. I understand they filmed *Dr. Doolittle* here.

"And Harold told me the coach can't go through the village because the roads are so narrow, so we'll be going in through the back way. I'm glad Harold has to drive this bus. These little roads are so tiny, I keep thinking we're going to get stuck."

Glenda giggled. "Me too. And when I look up suddenly I have to keep myself from screaming at Alex that he's on the wrong side of the road. Poor Alex, he has a tough life with me as a backseat driver."

Claire glanced over at Alex, head against the window, eyes closed, totally out of it. "It looks like he's really suffering." She liked Glenda.

"You know, Glenda, you sure did John Pederson a favor when you talked them all into joining you at the Dorchester Tea Dance. I was noticing yesterday on the barge how much younger and prettier Mary was looking now that she's more relaxed."

"Oh, we had such fun. You should have come Claire, you would have loved it."

"Well, I'm sure it's more fun to go to a tea dance when you have someone to dance with. That's one of the penalties of being single."

"Well, I'll just have to see if I can't do something about that. Look at all the material available." Glenda looked speculatively around the coach.

Claire laughed. "Thanks, Glenda, but really, no thanks. I don't have the time or energy at this point in my life."

"Time or energy? Really Claire, of course you do. There's nothing like a little love affair to give one a burst of energy."

Claire realized with dismay that she had inadvertently dropped a challenge and Glenda would be working on a match for her the rest of the trip. She dropped her voice to a whisper. "But my friend, wouldn't like it. He wasn't that pleased about me going off on this trip without him. He definitely wouldn't understand a love affair."

"Oh, of course, dear. I wondered how such an attractive woman as you could remain unattached." Glenda whispered back happily, Claire's imaginary lover satisfying her. "Oh, oh, I see Alex is stirring. I'd better go back or he'll think they left me back in Avebury."

Claire didn't feel the slightest qualm of guilt about her lie. It made Glenda happy and it couldn't hurt anyone. She gazed out the window thinking about her options for the afternoon, deciding suddenly that she would take advantage of the sun that had made its appearance during their stop at Avebury to take a swim. Then she might settle with her book over tea. She had only been in England for a few days but she had already discovered how civilized afternoon tea could be. It was a pleasant moment in the afternoon to reflect on the day and to gather energy. She wondered how complicated it would be, and of course how much it would cost, to serve tea to customers who were in the shop at 4:00. It might prove to be popular. She smiled, deciding to think about it seriously when she got back.

Then the bus broke through the trees into a fair sized car park. Jack was issuing instructions, pointing out the path to the reception area and assuring everyone that their luggage would arrive at their rooms about the same time they did. And even as Claire gathered up her belongings and followed the others she saw the bellmen arriving with carts to take the luggage Harold was removing from the opened bin.

* * *

The gardens were wonderful in the half-light of the evening. The scents hung heavily; the shadows were deep and mysterious. Claire had been lucky enough to be assigned a charming room on the third floor, instead of across the courtyard in one of the outside buildings as some of the group had been. She had come down early to make sure all the arrangements for the banquet were complete but was assured she wasn't needed, and so she had wandered out to the gardens for a stroll before dinner.

The house was huge and ornate, really more of a castle. The grand entrance hall, visible from the garden path she was on, was now the reception hall. She stared through the half light, imagining the carriages pulling up in the circular drive, the jeweled guests climbing the endless stairs to the wide porch while the lit torches defied the descending darkness and the sounds of the orchestra drifted out through the opened portals. It was like a

Merchant and Ivory movie. She sighed, longing for the romance of that era.

She laughed at herself, admitting wryly that if she had indeed been here at that time she would have most likely been one of the scullery maids, not one of the privileged ladies dancing the night away.

"...So stupid." The harsh words cut through the evening quiet destroying Claire's musing. She paused looking around for the source. Now the voice was quieter, somehow more threatening, and the words were no longer clear. She slipped through the greenery in the general direction of the sound and almost gasped at finding herself witnessing a confrontation between Arnie and Jack. Arnie's face was in the shadows; his hands, motioning nervously, were indications of his stress.

Jack's back was to her but his whole posture was so menacing Claire immediately bristled and crashed loudly into the little clearing intent on saving Arnie.

"What's happening here?" She demanded, looking pointedly at Jack.

He straightened up and turned towards her with a blank look.

"Problem?" Arnie echoed. "No, no problem." His face was now bright red with embarrassment.

"Why do you ask?" Jack's innocent look didn't convince Claire.

"Well for one thing it sounded like you were having an argument." Claire wasn't going to make it easy for him. She couldn't imagine what was happening.

"Uh, no. We were just talking about the golf game this afternoon." Arnie shifted uncomfortably. "Uh, I guess I better get going or I'll be late for dinner. See you in a bit,

Claire." He backed away. "And Jack, thanks for your advice." Then he turned and scurried towards the manor.

"So, what was it really about?" Claire scowled at Jack.

"Just what he said. I ran into him here and he was talking about a problem he was having with his swing on the 5th hole." He raised his eyebrows and smiled. "Do you play?"

At her head shake he continued, "Well then, no use in explaining the problem to you. Suffice to say, it cost him the game and I was able to give him a bit of advice to correct the problem." His grin dared her to dispute him.

Claire felt anger surging through her. She hated his pompous, belittling attitude. She had been on the receiving end of someone's assumption of superiority on too many occasions in her life. She became enraged when people treated her like milquetoast, so now she forgot her tack.

"Well, I'm so glad you were able to help him," she said softly. "I'd hate to disrupt this group again by changing the tour guide once again." She saw by the change in his eyes he understood.

"Of course, Jack, I'm not as experienced as you are but I do know that the most important feature of this tour is to make sure the group has a good time. I'm sure you agree. And as Arnie is an important part of the group, whatever you can do to make this trip pleasurable for him will certainly be appreciated."

"I hear you," he muttered, heading for the house.

He got the message but she decided she would watch him carefully. If he caused any problems she'd call the Kingdom Tours Office and report him. Maybe she shouldn't wait, she considered. Maybe she should just call tomorrow and insist that he be replaced. No, she realized, after only one day it was apparent the group was enthralled with him even if she was not. Well, she decided, she'd still keep a close eye on him.

She continued her stroll in the garden. Now night was almost upon them. The soft glow of lights marked the paths and highlighted the statues tucked into little nooks. She was looking forward to dinner because she never had time for the tea she had planned. She was so thrilled with Hilliary Hall she just had to look around and that led her to the little village of Castle Combe. Fortunately the residents tolerated the many visitors prowling through their tiny village, snapping pictures of flower bedecked cottages and the picturesque bridges over their wandering stream. But Claire wasn't so tolerant. She soon wearied of the people, and their cameras, and returned to the hotel with just enough time for a refreshing swim before getting ready for dinner.

It was fully dark when everyone had gathered in the hall. The costumed servants, towel draped over their arms, dramatically swept open the doors to the massive dining hall. Claire oohed and ahhed with the rest at the effect. Candles set in massive iron candelabras tucked into each corner lit the dim hall. Smaller replicas were placed at intervals down the length of a huge table. The fire at the far end crackled noisily, cheering the room, creating a feeling of an age long gone. The gaily clad serving wenches poured wine and mead with an enthusiasm matched only by the guests' thirst. A trio of musicians strummed in the corner while jesters and jugglers competed for the guests' attention. Their plates, platters really, were heaped time and time again with food not likely to ever be served in the chic restaurants of California. Pigeon tarts, steak and kidney pie, joints of wild boar, creamed onions, roasted potatoes and thick crusted brown bread were all followed by puddings and tarts and cakes beyond description. As the evening progressed the noise grew louder, the banter bolder, the musicians broke into song and the guests, encouraged by the servers, got up to dance a jig or two.

Claire kept her eye on Jack who flirted with the ladies and encouraged the men and even took Liz on a lively spin around the table at one point in the evening, giving everyone a brief respite from the flash of her camera.

Arnie seemed fine and was even atypically gregarious, but that could have been attributed to the mead he seemed to be so taken with. He avoided Jack and Claire but socialized with the rest with enthusiasm. Claire, watching him, almost convinced herself she was mistaken about the tone of the scene she had witnessed in the garden.

Claire skipped breakfast in order to sleep longer. The night before had been too much fun. It was hard to get going this morning. She found some comfort in finding she wasn't the only one straggling bleary-eyed to the coach.

This trip to Bath was starting early because a friend of Lucy's had arranged a private tour of the ornately tiled Roman Baths before the usual opening hours. They were going to be allowed behind the scenes where excavations were ongoing. Only one hundred years ago no one knew of the existence of these ancient baths lying under the floors of the city that had flourished since the time the first Romans settled on the site of the hot springs. It seemed unbelievable people living here could have forgotten their existence, but now the site was a continuously unfolding treasure trove as each layer peeled back to disclose new insights into the life and times of those ancient peoples.

None of their group was willing to miss this unique opportunity given them through Lucy's connections, although some looked worse for wear from the party the previous night.

After they finished in the baths the group was on their own to explore the town and pursue their own agenda. They each knew the departure time and the meeting place to get the bus back to Hilliary Hall. Anyone who missed it would have to get back before departure time in the morning or be left behind. It was the spirit of the Untour.

Claire had started off with some of the others wending their way through the flower-bedecked streets. But somewhere, during the course of the morning she wandered off down an alleyway, finding a group of shops better described as second-hand goods than the antiques they claimed, and ended up in another area of the pedestrian mall. She emerged from a particularly interesting store to find Rosa and Liz angrily squared off on the mall in front of her. At first she was tempted to duck back into the shop and hope they would go away. Rosa's face was red, contorted with anger. Liz's face was smug, almost righteous and very stubborn. They were creating quite a disturbance on the tranquil little street.

She resigned herself to stepping in. "Liz, Rosa, what's the matter with the two of you? You're causing a scene."

"Get her off my back. I have a job to do and I'm perfectly capable of doing it." Rosa pushed her furious words through gritted teeth causing Claire to step back from her as if to ward off a pending attack.

"I don't want your job. I just want to make sure that you do it." Liz's sanctimonious reply didn't even try to assuage Rosa's anger. "Lucy needs that information or her book won't meet the deadline. And frankly, I think you are not taking your job seriously enough. After all, I've helped my father through several deadline crises and I know what it's all about."

Claire realized with a sinking feeling the situation had gotten way out of hand. "Look, Liz, I was just going to get a bit of lunch. Come with me and let's talk about this." Claire held on to Liz's arm, restraining her, as Rosa stomped off in the other direction.

"Claire, really, let go of me!" Liz struggled but was no match for Claire's determined grip. "Look, I need to follow her. I have to go..." But when Rosa was no longer in view, she gave up, explaining further, "She really is up to something. I think she spends more time making assignments with men than she does gathering data for Lucy. She's not at all professional. She's..., well, she's a trollop!" This last was said with such seriousness that Claire felt her mouth fall open.

"Rosa? Come on, Liz. Aren't you exaggerating a little? Rosa certainly doesn't appear to be a...," she carefully kept her face straight, "...a loose woman." They sat down at one of the tables clustered outside a cheerful tearoom.

Liz didn't seem to notice the festive red geraniums bunched in window boxes and planters around the umbrella tables, nor did she even glance at the menus handed them. Instead she hunched forward looking straight into Claire's eyes. "This is no joke, Claire. Rosa isn't what she seems to be."

Claire was dismayed. She had to do something or Liz was going to ruin the whole trip. In spite of Lucy's assurances that Liz was only going thorough a period of adjustment, Claire thought there was a real possibility Liz had gone off the edge.

"Liz, Rosa is just what she appears to be. She is humorless, hardworking and very conscientious. Rosa came highly recommended by Lucy's publisher. He has worked with her several times over the years. And when it became obvious that Katy couldn't come back in time to meet the book's deadline he begged Rosa to take this assignment. She has relocated in order to be available to Lucy and she generously agreed to accompany us on this trip after Lucy had her accident. She does not consider this trip to be fun; to her it is her job. She is exactly what she seems to be, Lucy's assistant with exceptional skills." Claire spoke firmly and slowly, as if speaking to a child.

Liz stubbornly shook her head. "But I've seen her." Liz wouldn't give up. "At Camden Market and today. And I'm not with her all the time."

"What exactly did you see, Liz?"

"Well, she was making some assignment with a man." Liz sniffed righteously.

"Did you hear her?"

"Well, not exactly. But I could tell what she was doing. And then when I approached, he moved off real quick with a strange expression on his face." She shivered, her imagination now frightening her. "And that guy she was talking to at the market in London, she didn't want to be seen and she didn't want his picture taken."

"Liz, you're really stretching it." Claire was stern now. "Lucy has every confidence in Rosa. She has given her detailed instructions.

"And, Liz, did you know Rosa calls Lucy every few days to report and get additional information? Lucy has total control of the situation. She is directing Rosa's actions. You don't need to monitor Rosa, Liz. Lucy doesn't need it and Rosa doesn't like it.

"Liz, promise me you'll try to stay out of Rosa's way?" she coaxed, watching Liz's eyes, reading her objections.

"Liz, you came to see the country. There are twenty other people on this tour and they're all fun and interesting. Don't make Rosa your project. You're keeping her from doing her job."

Liz wouldn't agree so Claire sighed and added, "Liz, if you don't stop I'm going to have to send you back. I can't let you continue to disrupt this whole tour. It isn't fair to the others.

"Now, I'm serious about this. Are you listening? If I don't see some immediate improvement you're going back."

And she gave a final caution. "Remember that I mean it!"

* * *

The forest now crowded thickly around their path. A breeze rustled the leaves high above them and, always not far away, the sound of the brook they had crossed several times which was keeping up with them. It was like a concert—the rustle of leaves, the gurgle of water, the birds' songs, the occasional scolding of a squirrel. Claire was glad that Alice seemed as content as she was to just walk, letting nature restore their spirits.

She and Alice Jones had started out with several others a while ago, but the others were eager for a pint in the pub in Biddlestone where they planned to dine tonight so had taken a fork in the path almost an hour ago. She and Alice weren't quite ready to end their walk and elected to continue. It was perfectly safe, they assured the others. These were public access paths and clearly marked.

But they hadn't seen another person since they separated from the group. That might have been eerie but somehow it just added to the serenity. Now, however, Claire realized she was hungry and glanced at her watch. It was almost seven o'clock so she picked up her pace somewhat.

"Claire, I think this is our turnoff."

She looked at the map Alice was holding out to her and nodded her agreement. "Looks like it. I hate to leave the woods but my stomach has started complaining."

Alice laughed. "Well, I have to admit a pint of ale sounds good to me. That is, of course, if the rest have left us anything. They've had a good hour head start."

Claire felt a kinship with Alice, maybe because of their ages, maybe just because Alice was good company, like today on their walk in the woods. For a minute Claire considered asking Alice about Liz's behavior. Alice and Liz had elected to share a room to save money after meeting at one of the Untour orientation sessions. Surely Alice would have noticed if Liz was really becoming as erratic as she seemed.

No, she decided. She didn't think it fair to bring Alice into the loop of Liz's distressing behavior. Tomorrow she would talk to Rosa and once more to Liz and, if Liz didn't leave Rosa alone, she would then make arrangements to send Liz back. It was ridiculous she needed to be concerned about members of the tour causing nasty scenes in such pleasant surroundings as the pedestrian mall in Bath. What example of America was that to set?

Abruptly the path ended at the edge of a crammed car park. The King George Pub was obviously popular. Claire and Alice squeezed into the main room looking for friends when finally they saw Tom wave, loudly calling to them.

"We were just talking about sending out the search party but no one could agree on which way to go."

"Or even who should go."

Everyone laughed, pushing closer to make room for them to sit. Mugs of foaming, tepid ale appeared in front of them.

"We have our name in for a table. It won't be long now. The food is supposed to be good and judging by this crowd I would guess it is," Vern said, eyes on Mike playing darts with Glenda. He chuckled, nodding his head in that direction. "He likes to think he's tops at everything and Glenda has just whupped his sorry butt. Look, I think some of the locals want her to join their team."

His eyes crinkled in merriment at Mike's face. "Have a drink, lad. You were obviously playing out of your league."

"We put up a board in the den when the boys were little. Glenda is just a natural. No one will play her at home," Alex commented before asking Mike solicitously, "You didn't let her talk you into playing for money, did you?"

Mike squirmed at the laughter, not willing to admit how much he lost.

Alex leaned across the table. "Just a hint, young fellow. Don't ever play pool with her. Pool is her game."

At least half of their group had elected to eat at the Pub and it proved to be a good choice. Dinner was served in a room in the back where the host had shoved enough tables together for them. The floors were uneven from centuries of use. The ceilings were low and smoke darkened. Here, the noise was more subdued, and the smells tantalizing. The menu was eclectic, offering something for everyone. Claire bravely tried the veal chop, mostly because it sounded so English, but also because the menu noted it was raised naturally. Vern chose the duck in brandied cherry sauce, which, he said, was as tasty as it sounded. Several of the group chose the fish and chips and they all tasted the mashed peas, which turned out to be just that. Canned peas overcooked and mashed to a paste. No one would eat them after one taste and everyone was at a loss to understand the popularity of the item. After the "Pud," which the locals called dessert, Claire was one of the minority ready to head back. Vern and Mike decided to share the car they requested from Hilliary Hall, refusing to be baited by the others, who called them party poopers as yet another round of ale appeared.

"I had a hard enough time getting up this morning. I'd never make it two days in a row." Claire grimaced.

Vern chuckled. "You should have seen the jester here. He would stay to the last."

Mike nodded sheepishly. "What I wouldn't have given for a big Bloody Mary and a couple more hours of sleep this morning. That's turning out to be the trouble. I want to do everything and I'm finding that I can't. I hope age isn't catching up with me."

"Not a chance. It was that mead."

Vern and Mike were going to stroll around the grounds before having a nightcap, but Claire declined their invitation choosing to use a few quiet hours to finish her book on Stonehenge.

All thought of quiet hours disappeared when Rosa, her face even paler than usual, cut her off before she reached the lift.

"Oh Claire, I'm so sorry. It's terrible and all my fault." Rosa was actually wringing her hands.

"What are you talking about? What's happened?"

"Well, there's been a bit of an accident." Jack's calm voice didn't keep Claire's blood pressure from shooting to her brain, causing her head to pound in unison with her heart, almost drowning out his words.

"What? Who?" She knew it was terrible. Why else would Rosa be wringing her hands? Why else would Jack be so studiously calm?

Rosa wailed again, "It's all my fault. I didn't know she was there."

"Calm down, Rosa." Jack's voice cut her off. "It's Liz, Claire. She fell down the front steps as they were all going to catch their ride to the Dodington House this afternoon."

"Is she...? I mean..." Claire swayed at the horror of her thoughts but Jack's fingers gripped her arm steadying her. She pulled herself away sharply. "How serious is it?"

"Somewhat serious though certainly not life threatening. She's at the surgery now. She has broken her collarbone so I'm afraid she won't be able to continue the journey. They'll keep her here for about four days and then the manager of Hilliary Hall has offered to take her back to Heathrow and get her on a plane for the States.

"Hilliary Hall is very concerned of course. As they should be as it happened on their property. But it really was an accident. We were all going down the front steps. You know how steep they are. I can't imagine why they haven't put a railing up.

"Anyway, Rosa stopped and turned around to go back for something and didn't realize that Liz was right behind her. Liz apparently couldn't stop in time and tripped over Rosa. She fell all the way to the bottom. It happened so suddenly that no one else even saw what happened until she rolled past. Actually, I guess we're lucky she didn't knock anyone else down on her way to the bottom."

Claire shuddered, picturing half of the group being mowed down like bowling pins.

Rosa kind of moaned as Jack told the story. "It's all my fault. What will Lucy say? I tried to grab her, to save her but it happened so fast I couldn't get a good hold."

Claire took Rosa by the arm and shook her a little. "Rosa, stop this. It was an accident, just as Jack said. Now, stop blaming yourself and go have a warm drink, something like coffee laced with cream and brandy. Then go to bed and stay warm. I know it wasn't your fault. I'll call Lucy in the morning and explain it all. Don't worry!"

She saw Rosa attempt to compose herself and said more gently, "Go on now, and get a drink. That's an order." She watched Rosa turn towards the bar, calling after her, "Then go to bed."

She turned back to Jack. "I'll have to go see Liz and talk to the doctor. I appreciate all you've done but I need to see for myself. I'm sure you understand."

And she could see he did. He chose to be gracious, their past problems forgotten for the moment. "Of course."

"I just feel kind of funny about just leaving her here while we go on."

"Yes, but what else can you do? You can't cancel all the arrangements and everyone's plans for one person. That doesn't make sense. None of us can really do anything for her."

Claire nodded, now starting to feel annoyed. "Isn't that just like Liz? I had a serious talk with her this morning about leaving Rosa alone. She is always following her and now see what happened! And of course, Rosa blames herself but it was Liz's fault, I'm sure."

Jack took one of the hotel's cars, roaring through the dark lanes as if he could see beyond the glow of the lights, while Claire held on tightly, mentally selecting and discarding options. She arrived at the conclusion that if she survived this drive with Jack, it only made sense for the tour to go on. Just then Jack swerved to the side of the road in front of a cheery looking cottage, marked as the surgery by only a small plaque set on the gate. The room Claire was ushered into was very professional and scrupulously clean. Each of the four beds was set in such a way as to afford their occupants the most privacy. However, only one was occupied with the curtain drawn around it. Claire paused before approaching, looking for permission from Sister Strom.

"She's sedated and groggy but she's awake. At least she was a moment ago. She keeps asking for Claire. Is that you?"

Claire nodded, thinking, "Poor Liz."

Jack turned away with the sister. "I'll wait out here for you. Let me know if you need me."

Claire moved reluctantly forward, this whole scene too much like the one she had just played out when she visited Lucy in the hospital after her accident.

What was it with people and stairs? Why couldn't they watch where they were going?

Then she recognized her irritation for what it was, a minor form of panic and, forcing what she hoped was a cheerful smile, she pulled the curtain back to look at Liz.

"Claire? Claire, is that you?" Liz's voice was croaky, slurring slightly from the sedatives.

"Liz, how are you?" Her own voice was low and trembling.

"Claire, she pushed me. Rosa pushed me down the steps!"

"Liz, no!" Claire's voice was stronger now. "You tripped over her. She stopped and you were right behind her and you tripped."

"No, she pushed me. I tried to save myself. And I dropped my camera. I'm sure I've lost all the pictures I had on the film. I told you she didn't want me to be able to prove what she was doing."

Claire stooped over her, feeling very sad. "You're wrong, Liz. I told you this morning to leave her alone. You were right behind her again; right on her heels and when she stopped, you didn't and you fell over her. She tried to save you by grabbing you. That's probably why you're confused. It was an accident."

"Nooo, I fe... felt..." Her words faded and she seemed to sleep.

Claire and Jack went over all the arrangements with Sister Strom and then with the hotel manager back at Hilliary Hall. Then they called Lucy, as it was a more reasonable time in California than it was in England. With all that finished and arranged, Claire felt more confident. But then she remembered that Alice was rooming with Liz and probably didn't know what had happened.

"Alice, its Claire," she whispered with her knock. The door opened, to a disheveled Alice, who had obviously been asleep.

"What's wrong?"

"It's Liz. She had an accident."

Alice looked confused and then turned on the light squinting at the other bed. "I didn't even know she wasn't here. What happened? Is it serious?" She opened the door wider and Claire stepped in.

"Another set of stairs. She fell down the front steps on the way to her outing this afternoon and she broke her collarbone. Luckily it's not as serious as it is painful."

"My God, there must be twenty or thirty of those steps. She could have been killed. How did it happen? Can she go with us? Will we still leave tomorrow?"

"She tripped over Rosa," was Claire's terse reply.

Alice nodded, seeming to understand immediately how that could happen.

"She'll have to stay here for a few days and then they'll put her on a plane back. Lucy will send someone to the airport to meet her and get her settled. So we're leaving tomorrow as scheduled." Claire smiled remembering Lucy's instructions. "Lucy wouldn't let us delay the trip because of her accident, so of course she wouldn't consider a delay for Liz's."

Alice looked around the room with some confusion.

"Don't worry about her things. The hotel will take care of all that. Just pack up your stuff in the morning. But I'm afraid you've lost your roommate for the remainder of the trip."

Since Alice didn't look sad at that thought, Claire suspected Liz was no more congenial as a roommate than she was a traveling companion.

Claire didn't bother to tell anyone of Liz's bizarre accusations, certain that when Liz was more herself she would have a clearer understanding of what had really caused the accident.

And later, just before she went to sleep, Claire acknowledged her own relief at Liz's departure. She was an odd duck. She just didn't fit into the group. In her heart she knew she would have had to send her home at some point. And as much as she was unhappy Liz had been hurt, it would be a more enjoyable trip for them all without her.

CHAPTER SIX

The other members of the tour were appropriately concerned over Liz's injury but none seemed to question the decision to leave as scheduled. Claire was grateful she didn't have to do much explaining. Apparently Alice, Jack and the others on the scene of the accident had spread the word. Mrs. Maus sat with Rosa for a while, either to provide comfort or to show support, so at least Rosa seemed calm this morning and now was absorbed in her computer screen.

If Claire had been groggy yesterday morning, this morning she was almost numb from sleep deprivation.

"How about a cuppa while we go over the agenda?"

Claire looked up. Seeing Jack's proffered cup, she moved over to the seat next to the window before taking the hot cup from him. He certainly looked chipper this morning, but then this was his business. He must be used to these hours, this traveling. Settling back, she took a sip, relaxing as the milk and sugar laced tea did its work. At first she had found the tea to be a disgustingly different drink than the Chinese and herbal teas she was used to drinking. But now she enjoyed the hearty brew with both milk and sugar.

"Did you get any sleep?" Jack's concern was new. He actually sounded as if he cared. They had yet to overcome the ill feelings resulting from that initial meeting in the stairwell. Of course the incident in the garden with Arnie hadn't helped mend the rift.

"Not much," she admitted. "You?"

"As much as I need. I'm not much of a sleeper."

"Really, is that how you keep up with these tours? I don't know how you do it. Harold just seems to disappear whenever we stop, appearing magically with the bus, I mean coach, at just the right time. But you are with us and still seem to be ahead of us."

"It's the training you know. And we have our trade secrets." His grin suggested something risqué, as he pulled out the itinerary.

After he had refreshed Claire's memory on the activities scheduled for that day and the next, she couldn't help asking, "How long have you been doing this?"

"Not long. It pays the bills and it's fun. So for now, it's okay."

Claire looked at his weathered face, guessing him to be about her own age. She was curious, wondering about his life before Kingdom Tours but, not willing to risk being rude, she decided not to ask.

Jack answered anyway. "I was a history teacher but I became redundant. So, this seemed to be a good thing."

"Redundant?" Claire was confused.

"Yes, you know. The job went away. What do they call it in the States?"

Now she saw his meaning. "Downsizing or something similar. Redundant, what an interesting way to describe it."

"Actually, I took my degree in engineering, but I was redundant there first. So I pursued my love of history to support me. It seemed a very safe choice. There was a time when English history was important, but no longer." He sounded very sad.

"There you have it. That's the bloody British Empire in the twenty-first century. We're all redundant but either don't know it or won't admit it." His cynicism was a sharp departure from his usual cheeky but cheerful manner.

"That's terrible. Weren't you able to get another engineering position?"

"Not without leaving the country, and I didn't want to be so far away from my daughter."

"Oh, I didn't realize you were married. Well, all this traveling must be difficult for your family." She wondered why she was surprised to learn he was married.

He crooked his eyebrow. "Not really. I'm not married. I was many years ago, and when I first became redundant, my daughter was only twelve. And, while I could only see her at specified times, it seemed important for both of us that I shouldn't just give that up. So teaching looked like a good solution. And now she's grown and off on her own, and we can see each other whenever we want. So now I have the freedom to do what I want.

"What about you? Do you do this for a living? What about husbands, children, etc.?"

"No, no and no. I was a librarian." She paused while he nodded his agreement. She knew everyone thought she was a teacher but when they heard she was really a librarian, they always nodded like this. Of course, the nod said, she looked just like a librarian. And not Marian the Librarian from *The Music Man* either.

"Anyway, a few years ago I inherited my Uncle's bookstore in a little town outside of San Francisco, and I decided to make it into something fun." She smiled at the memory. "Everyone said I was crazy, it was too risky, but I had this idea about a travel bookshop. I suppose my name influenced me because, other than armchair adventures, I have never traveled."

She laughed softly. "I confess I can be a little headstrong. So I did it and it worked. Lucy Springer and I became friends after she did a couple of lectures at the shop to promote her books. When she thought up this trip I agreed to co-sponsor it. And here I am."

"That sounds like you left a lot out! Weren't you nervous giving up a secure career for something so iffy? I mean I was forced out twice. I had to make a change, albeit kicking and screaming like everyone else. You just did it for a lark?" Jack looked puzzled and maybe a little envious.

Claire shrugged. "Not really. Something had happened to me before my Uncle died that made me rethink my whole safe, secure life. I guess by the time I got the bookstore, I was ready to take a few chances, to live a little.

"Do you remember Auntie Mame's character, Agnes Gooch? '*I wanna live!*'" She waited for his nod. "Well, something like that. Fortunately, so far it has turned out a little better for me than it did Agnes." She finished her tea, not willing to discuss or even think about the incident which changed her life and still gave her nightmares.

Jack took the hint and the cup. "Well, I better get ready, we'll be leaving the M-5 soon, and the folks will want their tour guide patter."

Claire stared out the window at the motorway, watching the cars pass them on the wrong side, steeling herself not to jump. She wished she hadn't mentioned that long ago incident. She saw the interest flare in his eyes. She just didn't want to think about it.

Unfortunately, the nightmares never let her completely forget it, and she had experienced a rerun only last night during the few hours she slept. Maybe Liz's irrational accusations about Rosa had brought on the dream. She hadn't been deeply asleep when the nightmare started. Her subconscious had struggled with the petrifying fear, refusing to give in, and she had woken herself up before the worst part, as she was sometimes able to do. Afterwards she couldn't rid herself of that feeling of terror, so she finally got up and made a cup of tea from the electric kettle in her room. Then she was nervous about going back to sleep for fear she would have to finish the dream. She had been glad when morning finally came with the rush of departure chores to distract her.

Gradually, Jack's voice penetrated her thoughts and she realized he was describing the countryside and the River Wye, which they had just crossed and would several times more before the day was done. She realized she liked him a little better today but she wondered, uncomfortably, if she only felt that way because she had learned that he was educated and was capable of holding a more responsible position than that of a tour guide.

No, he was a likeable guy. Everyone in the group thought so, even if she didn't. But there was something that didn't quite compute about Jack. Something about him made her antennae quiver. She still didn't fully trust him, and she still didn't believe his and Arnie's story about the golf game. She had heard the anger in his voice. But why would he be angry with Arnie, the most harmless soul on this tour? Then she gave it up, concentrating instead on Jack's description of Hay-on-Wye, their next destination.

* * *

"We thought we'd have to leave without you, Claire. You know, *promptly*?"

"Thought you got lost."

"Guess you were having a good lunch?"

"Must've found a better pub than we did."

"Come on, I've got two minutes. I didn't come even close," she retorted good-naturedly to the jibes, relieved to see Vern had made it to the bus before her.

Vern and Claire had spent all their available time in the numerous bookstores for which the picturesque Hay-on-Wye was famous. They combed through the musty, endless hodgepodge shelves of used books. Claire had selected some old travel books she thought she'd add to her stock at the shop, thinking customers may have fun reading about travel from another time and comparing those adventures to today's world. And of course, she couldn't resist a few for herself, including some she brought with her to read on the trip. Vern had finally left Claire to make arrangements to have her books shipped while he went off to find something for their lunch.

She dropped down in the seat across from Vern and Mike. "I thought I'd beat you."

"Hardly." He held up a bulky bag proudly. "I thought some sustenance would be in order." He pulled down the little tray table from the back of the seat in front of his and started to unload his bag. Vinegar Crisps, England's answer to potato chips, hunks of heavy brown bread, a soft blue

Brie and a harder yellow cheese came out. He carefully unwrapped a slab of delicious smelling terrine and a small container of olives. “See if Jack’s got some knives in that little closet of a kitchen he has back there, and some of those plastic glasses he uses for serving.” He called after her, “Bring extra glasses. I have enough to share.”

By the time Claire returned, Vern had the cork out of the bottle of wine. The wine wouldn’t have gone very far, but it was miraculously supplemented from bottles stashed in backpacks and tote bags up and down the aisle. Soon a party was in full swing. Jack forgot his spiel for once and even Rosa left her computer to join the group. When the coach arrived at Llandyn Wells, they were all in fine spirits. Claire made it to her room and collapsed on her bed.

“Claire, Claire. Are you there?”

She stumbled to the door trying to compose herself, disoriented from her deep sleep. She opened the door to Alice’s anxious face. “I fell asleep,” she explained lamely.

Alice laughed. “You weren’t the only one. Not too many made it down to dinner.

“Look, I know you didn’t get much sleep last night, so I was hesitant about waking you. But it’s almost time for that Variety Show that Jack was so enthusiastic about. I thought I should check to see if you wanted to come.”

“Oh, thanks, Alice. I do want to go. Lucy said it was great. That’s why we had to be here on Wednesday. So we wouldn’t miss it.” She motioned Alice in, hurrying to open her bag which was still sitting by the door. “Who’s going?” she asked as she darted into the bathroom.

“Everyone from dinner and I guess anyone who wakes up in time. Mike and Vern, and the Sorini’s are waiting downstairs for us. It’s only a ten minute walk.”

"Let me find an aspirin and I'm ready." Indeed, face washed, hair brushed and teeth cleaned she looked normal. "You know, Alice, I swear I didn't have that much wine."

"Obviously it was enough," was the droll reply, and they were both still giggling when they joined the others in the lobby.

Claire was glad for the warmth of the Naval jacket she purchased in Camden Market, as they walked through the cool, dark streets. Ornate Edwardian streetlamps glowed orange, barely making a dent in the dark shadows cast by the gargoyles and serpents decorating the towering old brick buildings. The streets slanted gently down to the park's entrance and then winding paths led to the bathhouses built for another era when this was a famous spa town and the gentry converged here to take the waters and mingle. The theatre sat amongst the bathhouses designed in the same style. It had been updated but only superficially. The lights were electric, instead of gas, and the required exit signs and fire escapes had been added. Otherwise it looked and felt like it came from another century.

"Is this everyone?" Jack was waiting in the lobby.

"I don't know. Vern said Mrs. Maus, the sisters, Joe and Warren left ahead of us," Claire replied, waving the others on while she went over the tour members with Jack, feeling somewhat remiss in performing her responsibilities.

"Yes, they're here, and the Mohney's, and Kim and Annie."

"So who is missing?" Claire grimaced. The pain was not gone from her head and it was making her a little confused. Jack's amused expression at her discomfort annoyed her. She was sure she hadn't had that much wine.

Obviously his head was functioning fine because he counted off, "By my reckoning the Pederson's, Glenda and Alex, Arnie, Betty and Rosa. Do you want me to wait for them?"

"No, Joan told me that John and Mary weren't coming. Rosa is probably working to make up for playing with us this afternoon. I don't know where Arnie, Betty or the Martinez's are, but they must have decided to skip it." She handed her ticket to the young man at the door, took a program and went into the theatre. Mrs. Maus had saved some seats. She sat down next to Joe, greeting the others, then settled back, surprised to find that Jack had followed her in and was sitting on her other side.

"I didn't realize you wanted to see it too. I thought you'd be bored as often as you do these things."

"Not by this show. Just wait."

It was obviously a small town production where the smaller children of the players handed out the playbills and the older and the spouses moved the props. When the first skit started, the broad accents were so confusing that Claire glanced toward the exit wondering if she could leave without being noticed. But unconsciously her ears seemed to adjust and she found herself laughing as hard as anyone. The comedy was universal; the players' timing skills could have competed in any major city in the world. Skit after skit was presented and, in between the audience's tears of mirth, the Welsh tenors' poignantly sad songs brought tears of another kind to their eyes. Not knowing the language of the songs didn't hamper the audience's enjoyment. When it was over, they applauded, stood and clapped some more, reluctant to end the evening, knowing they would never see the equal of this show again.

Claire followed some other ladies into the loo and patiently waited her turn. When she came out, the lobby was nearly empty and none of the tour members were around, not even on the steps where a few people lingered. She felt deserted but then shrugged off her uneasiness. After all, there were others on the street. She reminded herself that this small remote town wouldn't have any of the big city dangers she was used to. But she was still a half block from the park's entrance when she became aware of the footsteps behind her. She speeded up, looking around for those others she had seen on the street only minutes ago. Her heart started to pound. She was scared and just about ready to break into a totally undignified run.

"Hey, slow down a minute and I'll walk back with you." Jack caught up to her and slipped his arm through hers as if they were friends. "How did you get out here by yourself? It's not smart, you know? A good looking woman walking a dark lonely street by herself is an invitation for trouble."

Claire could be cool now that her heart was beating normally again. "Well, I must have spent too much time in the loo. Everyone was gone when I came out. But, surely it's safe in a little town like this."

Jack stopped abruptly turning her towards him. "Lady, what country did you say you're from? There is no place in the world that is safe." The light casting shadows on his stern face emphasized his words and caused Claire to shiver. He moved up the street, still holding her arm. "But, this place is probably safer than most," he conceded.

"You know, Claire, I'd like to meet your Lucy Springer sometime. This is one of the most unusual tours I've been on. She's hit so many of my favorite spots, I'm looking forward to the ones she's selected that I haven't even heard about. I'm sure I'd like her."

They talked about Lucy and the book she was writing until he bid her goodnight in the lobby, reminding her with a gentle smile, "Remember, 8:30 promptly. And stay out of the service stairwells. I'll be collecting the luggage with Harold tomorrow."

Claire hummed some of the songs from the show while she got ready for bed. It had been a wonderful day and she was looking forward to the next. Now that Liz wasn't there to cause friction it looked as if the tour would just get better and better.

And Jack wasn't so bad. Maybe she had misjudged him. After all, Arnie seemed okay with him. Why should she be so suspicious? Claire slept soundly that night and if she dreamed she didn't know it.

* * *

Hotel Victoria
Llandyn Well, Wales

Day 6--Wednesday

Dear Lucy,

This was a great day. Maybe for me the best yet, but you know how I love books and the theatre is indescribable.

Rosa's doing well, has settled in now that Liz has left and even joined our impromptu party on the bus today. Tour guide, Jack, is working out fine in spite of my concerns. I think you'd like him. I'm glad we came. You were right; we can do it.

Hope you're doing okay and the pain is subsiding. See you soon.

Love, Claire

Lucy Springer
123 5th Street
Burlingame, CA 94010
U.S.A

AIR MAIL

* * *

“They had a casualty. Liz Cooley fell down the steps at Hilliary Hall and has been left behind.” Fenster couldn’t resist adding the drama of a pause. “And she says Rosa pushed her.”

“Why?”

“Liz says that Rosa has been meeting men all along the way, and Liz was able to capture two of them on film. Liz says Rosa’s afraid that Liz will report her to her boss. So she got rid of her by pushing her down the stairs when no one was looking.”

Ames’ smile was terrifying. No wonder the man had become such a power. “That’s it? Who are the men? Why the meetings? And, where are the pictures she took?”

Fenster shrugged. “The camera was broken and the film ruined in her fall. We went through her things but didn’t find any more film. So that must have been all she took. Of course, we’re checking on Rosa already. The information will be coming.”

“What about your agent on the tour?”

“Actually, he’s very skeptical of Liz’s story. Says she might be balmy—change of life problems or something.”

“I’ll expect some real information soon, Fenster. Make sure I get it.”

Fenster made his way to his own office, several floors below, mulling the Rosa angle. What, why, who? It just didn’t compute with what he already knew. But he was experienced enough to know they would check every angle completely and assume nothing.

CHAPTER SEVEN

Claire rifled through her backpack and, finally finding the book, she moved down the aisle to sit across from George and Florence. “Hey, George, I found this at one of those bookstores yesterday and thought you’d like it.”

He took the battered volume, turning it over in his hands.

“You’ve read Dick Francis, haven’t you? I think this is a first edition, even though it’s pretty tattered. It’s one of his early novels and I thought you might appreciate it.”

George nodded, obviously touched. “Aw, Claire, I can’t take this. I mean, I’d like to read it, but it may be valuable. I’ll just borrow it from you.”

“No, I bought it for you. That store didn’t even know what they had. I don’t think its worth much to a serious collector. It doesn’t even have the dust jacket, but I had to buy it. It really is a treasure for someone who reads mysteries. I don’t, and I know you do.”

“You don’t read mysteries? But how do you know so much about them? You even know the characters?” He was clearly puzzled.

"I used to be a big fan. I craved mysteries. When I worked at the library I read them all. Then one day I just didn't want to read them any more," Claire admitted.

"Just like that?"

She nodded. "Just like that! Maybe they became too real for me, so they weren't fun anymore. That's about the time I started reading travel books. Travel books are interesting but benign. You know, they don't make your heart leap with fear." She smiled and continued, "And you know where that interest led me."

Florence chuckled. "Well, thank goodness you didn't open your shop earlier, or it might have been Sherlock's Book Shop, and we'd be running through the streets of London with magnifying glasses wearing tattersall cloaks." Her eyes sparkled with merriment.

George was already thumbing through the book, anxious to start it. So Claire worked her way down the aisle stopping here and there to talk, arriving at her seat just as the coach pulled into the car park at Powis Castle.

Those tour members who had spent their afternoon in the Pub at Castle Combe, instead of visiting the Dodington House and Gardens, now got their first glimpse of the grandeur of British living. The ornate furnishings, the collections of stuffed birds, china, leather and gold-tooled books, paintings, ivory and every imaginable knickknack were awesome. This wealth of possessions could fill a museum and it all belonged to a single family, who kept adding wings to their dwelling over the centuries in order to accommodate more of the possessions they acquired.

The estate was so vast it was impossible to explore more than a small portion in the time they had allotted. The gardens were laid out so the view from every window of the manor house would be pleasing to the eye and yet, tucked in amongst the flowers, were vegetables and fruit, planted in such a way as to enhance the beauty of the garden and still feed the household.

The next stop was at a little pub in the middle of nowhere, but they seemed to be expected. Hearty bowls of soup and the ploughman's lunch consisting of coarse bread, cheeses, fruits and pickled vegetables were served and the group did well by it. In a remarkably short time they were on the road again, headed for the peaks of Snowdonia looming blue against the horizon.

The coach wound through bleak mountains of what looked like slate, as colorless as the clusters of cottages that marked each mine they passed. It was hard to imagine what life could be like for the inhabitants of these villages. No trees, no gardens, nothing it seemed would grow in the stripped terrain. What were the children like? In fact, where were the children? The inhabitants seemed to be missing and, except for an occasional cat lying in the sun on a windowsill and the wash hanging limply from the lines, the villages could have been deserted. It was very depressing. Maybe even more so after seeing the grandeur of Powis Castle earlier. Here was the source of the wealth that built the castles, that bought the collections and that maintained the gardens of the wealthy.

After the shock of the first village, they had a heated discussion which ended with Vern reminding them all of the razed mountains in Washington and Oregon where the logging industry had left landscapes almost as desolate. That silenced the coach. So it was a sober group of travelers who entered the boundaries of the Snowdonia where the greenery and unspoiled beauty still didn't erase the depression generated from the sight of the mining communities they had just passed.

The sudden stop woke them all up. Teacups and glasses flew along with anything that was not strapped down, including Betty, who was getting a drink of water. And Jack, who was always after them to keep their seatbelts fastened whenever possible, catapulted down the aisle grabbing ineffectually at seat rails until he crashed near Harold's seat and managed to right himself.

"What the bloody hell is going on?" Jack spoke for them all.

"Sorry, folks. It seems we have a problem up here." Harold hardly ever spoke, usually only nodding to Jack's comments.

Jack peered over Harold's shoulder. "I guess so!

"Got you're blinkers on? Better give me the emergency flashers." Then quickly assessing the chaos in the coach, he called out, "Mike, Warren, can you help me with these?" The two men hurried to the front and squeezed through the narrow opening between the coach door and the cliff, around the front of the bus and then back down the road to put the warning flashers on the road behind them.

Harold's sudden stop had been a shock. When they realized a crash was not going to follow, they quickly took an inventory of each other and found no one seriously hurt. Tom helped Betty to a seat and Annie headed for the kitchenette for some ice to put on Betty's arm where it was bruised and already swelling up. Other people were gathering up belongings and mopping up spilled drinks, setting things in order again.

They had been traveling on a road, which hugged the high cliff on the left, and the right side was bound by a low stone wall erected to prevent an inadvertent slip over the side to the river far below. The narrow road allowed barely enough room for cars to pass the coach. Directly in front of them, not even two-car lengths distance, a huge lager lorry, beer truck as the Americans would say, overlapped their space by about three feet. While the lorry might have been able to squeeze a little closer to the stone wall, there was just not enough space to allow the truck and bus to pass each other.

Claire peering through the front window saw the lorry driver climb down. She raised her voice and quickly explained the situation to the others on the coach. Then she squeezed out the door between the coach and the cliff and hurried to join what appeared to be a heated conversation developing on the road.

"How does this happen?" she murmured in Jack's ear as he stood to one side while the two drivers argued about who should back up. "Don't they post the widths? In the States we mark the roads for the truck drivers, so they can take alternate routes if necessary."

Jack just shook his head, his patience obviously taxed at her stupidity. "What alternative routes? These roads were here when people only walked and they were plenty wide enough. Actually this is a good road. You saw that one we went down to reach Castle Combe. Did you see a sign posted there? Drivers just have to keep their eyes open and use common sense to work it out."

Warren and Mike joined them as did several of the drivers from the vehicles beginning to stack up behind in each direction. Everyone had an opinion on how to solve the dilemma.

"The last turn out I passed was at least a mile back and uphill." The lorry driver was not going to back up.

"Look, if you guys would move to the same side of the road, we could take turns getting our cars around you," an impatient motorist offered.

"Sure, we'd stay here all day waiting for all the cars to get around until the next lorry or coach came along, and then it would be even worse. No, wait your turn. We'll get this sorted out," the lorry driver retorted angrily.

The other drivers protested loudly. Then Jack spoke with surprising authority and quieted them all.

"All right, keep calm. We're going to work this out. There was a turnout on the river side about a half mile back, right?" Several motorist nodded, having come that way themselves.

"So, we're going to back up the coach, one car length at a time. The car behind will go around the coach and pass through the space between the bus and the lorry. The lorry will continue to come forward, keeping the appropriate space between us, so we can keep clearing the cars behind us. When the coach backs past the turnout, the lorry can pull into it enough to let us pass, and then we'll all be on our way. Right?"

Everyone nodded agreement, relieved to have a plan. The drivers hurried back to their cars behind the bus, ready to get around the obstruction as soon as possible. The drivers behind the lorry seemed reconciled to their wait, but determined to follow the lorry closely to gain every foot available to them.

Jack turned the group into an army, assigning each a role in directing the traffic. Several moved down the right lane instructing the drivers in the left lane as to what the plan was, so they would wait for their turn instead of following the car in front of them cutting off the coach's retreat. Jack positioned himself against the cliff, behind the bus, using hand signals to direct Harold. Harold read Jack's directions in his mirror as he backed the coach fitfully down the narrow, curving road, one car length at a time.

It was working very well. Mary and Joan would block off the second car back, while John, Vern and Mike directed the car directly behind the coach, around and then back to the empty lane in front of the coach where it would speed gratefully off, happy to be free. Jack would then direct Harold back to the next car. Mrs. Maus, leaning lightly on her cane, Joe at her side, led the huge lorry as if it were a docile elephant, lumbering forward at a pace that allowed space for the autos moving out of the coach's way to pass. Some of the other tour members spread out behind the lorry to make sure the drivers didn't become impatient and try to pass, blocking the freed cars coming from the other direction. The rest of the tour members walked back towards the turnout, stopping to explain to the stalled drivers what was happening ahead.

Claire saw a car pulled halfway out of the line several cars back. Rosa was standing in front of the car. "What's going on?" Claire asked Terri.

"That driver thought he could jump the line." Terri grinned. "But Rosa saw him and cut him off."

"Does she need help?" Claire saw the man's angry expression and Rosa's hand waving him back, refusing to budge from his way.

Terri watched a minute before answering, "I wouldn't think so. She seems to have him under control."

And Claire saw as she passed on her way to the turn out that the man was calmer, now chatting with Rosa in a friendly manner, seemingly content to wait his turn to pass the coach. She couldn't help thinking that if Liz was here, she would be snapping Rosa's picture again, certain there was some clandestine motive for Rosa's conversation with the driver.

A spontaneous cheer signaled the turnout had appeared around the next curve in the road.

"Claire," Jack called down the road to her, "can you get everyone organized? When the lorry pulls over, we need everyone back on the coach but me, Mike and Warren, so we can get out of here before we get run over."

"Tom, did you hear Jack? Pass the word on down there. I'll go this way." Tom nodded reluctantly. He had been recording the whole episode on his video camera and, while he recognized the importance of passing on the message, he was loath to give up even one minute of film coverage.

Everyone squeezed back on the coach while both Jack and Harold directed the lorry driver into the little space hanging precariously over the river. The turnout was small, designed for a car with a problem not a tank-sized lorry, but it allowed enough space for the lorry to pull over slightly. Jack, Mike and Warren positioned themselves in front and behind. Tom was up the road with his camera while Harold, back in the driver's seat, moved slowly to pass. Everyone held their breath when the mirrors of the two vehicles tangled. Then the bus mirror flexed and they cleared the lorry, moving up the road a few yards to stop for the rest to climb aboard.

After the horns stopped their salute, the lorry pulled back into his lane. Harold headed out and they were on their way again. Kim and Annie took over Jack's job, distributing cold drinks and tea to the tired group. They all were very aware that each curve of the road could bring more surprises, but finally they left the narrow confines of the cliff road and Harold could drive with more confidence and speed. When Harold pulled into the car park at Gwynedd Hall in Conwy two hours late, they gave him a rousing cheer. The group insisted they would unload the luggage bins for the waiting hotel workers. Harold should rest. And if he had taken everyone up on their offer to stand him a couple at the local, he wouldn't have been in any shape to drive them next day for sure.

* * *

"Hi, Arnie. Did you get some dinner?" Claire ran into him as she was hurrying into their hotel lobby.

"Uh, just going. Did you?"

"Yeah, I went with Alice and the Martinez's. We had fish and chips down the street, that way. It was pretty good. But I saw a photo shop down on the next block that will develop pictures overnight, and they open early enough for me to get them before we leave tomorrow. So I came back to get my film. I'm meeting the others later at the Black Swan down by the wall, if you want to join us."

"Well," Arnie was squirming, his face pink, "Actually, I'm having dinner with Betty. So, I guess not. But, would it be an imposition to take some of my film? I'll pick it up in the morning. I have this new camera and I'm not sure how good I'm doing with it?"

"No problem. I'm going up to get my film. I'll meet you back down here in a few minutes."

It turned out Arnie had four rolls, which Claire dropped off with her two. Then as she headed down the street to the pub she tried to imagine Arnie and Betty as a couple. Betty was so glamorous. Her hair was always perfectly arranged, her nails long and red, and so far she appeared to have an endless wardrobe. Claire couldn't imagine how she could have gotten so many outfits in their limited luggage. Arnie, on the other hand, was disheveled, his hair looked as if he needed a cut and his nails were sometimes bleeding from his gnawing. And his wardrobe seemed to consist of the identical trousers and shirts, always slightly rumpled, worn with his favorite jacket, maroon, with his company's logo emblazoned in big letters across the back.

She smiled, thinking that maybe the unlikely duo would end up in a romance. Wouldn't that just tickle Glenda Martinez's matchmaking aspirations? And she was still grinning when she entered the smoky, dark pub.

"Did you come alone? I thought I just warned you to stay off dark streets." The gruff voice in her ear gave her a start.

"Oh, Jack, you startled me. But no one else was around. I know it's safer in numbers but I didn't want to miss the fun. Besides, I grew up in San Francisco. I'm street smart."

His skeptical look didn't buy her excuse but he let it go. "What are you drinking? I'm buying the first round for everyone, or at least Kingdom Coach Tours is. It's kind of a thank you for all the help today."

"That's really not nec...." She started to protest but changed her mind at seeing the determined look on his face. "How nice. I think I'll have a half and half." She had found that a glass of half bitter and half ale was more to her taste than a glass of either.

He nodded turning towards the bar while Claire moved to the back to join the others squeezed into the corner near the fire.

She was on her second when Terri leaned towards her. "Look, Claire. Isn't that the guy on the road who tried to breach the line?"

Claire squinted through the gloom and, after studying the guy Terri had pointed at, she nodded. "I think so. He was in such a hurry then and he's ended up in the same place we did anyway."

"Well, I'm going to buy him a drink." Mike grinned, feeling no pain. "If he was tamed by Rosa he can't be a danger to me."

The others hooted at him as he swaggered across the room. Then they lost sight of him in the milling crowd.

"Not a very friendly American. Didn't want a drink, didn't want to chat, just got up and left," Mike reported back in a wounded tone.

"Don't worry, sweetie." Shar patted his arm, pulling him down to the stool beside her. "We know enough Americans. We're here to meet Englishmen!"

"Welsh!"

"Huh?"

"We're in Wales. If we want to meet the locals, they'd be Welshmen, not Englishmen."

Shar shrugged at her sister's clarification turning instead to tell Mike a joke about a Welshman and an Irishman, which improved Mike's mood considerably.

When Mrs. Maus, Joe, and the Martinez's announced they were going back to the hotel, Claire decided to join them, leaving the diehards to party on.

The dark fog enveloped them, muffling their footsteps as they hurried up the slick street. Except for the occasional streetlamp, they could have been in another era. Claire shivered violently, feeling the goose bumps move from her scalp down her back.

"Someone stepped on a grave, my mother used to say," Mrs. Maus told her.

"Not a pretty thought on a night like this," Claire answered, glad to see their hotel looming up in front of them. This day had been long enough for her.

* * *

"Hello." The figure materialized out of the darkness, the swirling fog blurring his features.

"Christ, you gave me a fright. What are you doing up here?"

"Same as you, I expect. It is a little eerie, isn't it? Lucy is right about this place and seeing as we got here so late I thought I'd just take a walk before turning in." He peered intently ahead. "By the way, I thought I heard voices. Was one of the other members of the tour up ahead?"

"Voices? No, just a man passing; looked like he was a local. Maybe he just wanted a respite from his family or a quiet smoke. Well, I'm going down. It's too dark and dangerous up here. You coming?"

"No, I think I'll walk a little further, maybe come down near that pub the others are at. Want to come?"

"No, I've had enough. Let me get by you." The two moved carefully to pass each other, mindful of the crumbling inner edge, the fog slicked stones and the long way down to the houses gathered below.

In passing, the inner figure nudged the dark figure at the edge, throwing him slightly off balance. Arms flailing, he reached out for a steadying hand, but instead a foot slammed into his knee and sent him over the edge. His cry of horror, muffled by the wetness in the swirling air, was abruptly silenced by an ominous thud. The remaining figure hurried on, now hurrying to get off the wall.

CHAPTER EIGHT

The fog still hung thick and wet but it wasn't going to deter her. She was going to walk on the old wall surrounding the town. Lucy had sent them here because of this high wall. It enclosed the town, which huddled against the base of the castle, just as it had for seven hundred years. Later they would see York with its famous wall, but Lucy dismissed York with "very picturesque." Conwy, she said, was the wall to see.

Claire was out early and had picked up the pictures first thing, paying for Arnie's too. She stuffed them in the side pouch of her backpack, and then skimmed through hers as she headed for the stairway on the wall. But once there, the pictures were forgotten. She ascended the steep, rough staircase carefully. At the top she paused, shrouded in fog, all sound muffled, as she then carefully picked her way along. At this height the wind swirled the dense clouds, allowing views in snatches of the dripping roofs far below; the bay stretching to the north and west; and an occasional seagull, gliding past on the air currents.

In places where the wall had crumbled dangerously, the town had built little bridges with handrails to protect the tourists. But the rest was left weathered and rough just as it had been built. The crenelled wall looked like a castle wall should. The cutouts were used by the archers to repel any attackers. The inner edge was a ledge of stone about a foot high. In some places the walkway had deteriorated to the point that it was barely wide enough for two people to pass carefully. Claire shuddered, wondering how many had escaped the enemy arrows only to perish by falling over the inner edge, disoriented by the fatigue of battle.

The fog had definitely started to burn off by the time she approached the elbow where the wall turned to run along the bay. Ahead she saw several people grouped, excitedly pointing down at something. She approached them curiously and then followed their pointing to the rooftop below. It looked like a crumpled rag. Then she gasped.

"What happened? How did it happen?" She was so horrified she didn't even register the answers swarming around her. She clutched a stranger as she searched for answers. "Did anyone see him fall? Did anyone call an ambulance?"

Just then the ambulance and the police arrived. Ladders were found and rescue workers started climbing to the roof. She didn't know how she got down from the wall, but she was pushing through the crowd, aware that the group on the wall above her was growing as others climbed up for a better view.

"Hey, hold on there. This is police business, Miss. Please stand back."

"But it's Arnie. He's with us. I mean he's a member of our tour. I'm in charge. I have to do something." She knew she wasn't quite coherent but the policeman apparently understood and he led her over to two men standing to the side, one talking on a mobile phone directing the rescue efforts on the roof. It was apparent from his conversation that there was no hope of Arnie having survived that fall.

The older man was very kind and obviously experienced at this, because it wasn't long before he had gotten her story in some semblance of order, had her sitting in the police van with a cup of bracing tea and then, a short time later, he and another man transported her to the police station for further questioning.

"Oh, my God! What time is it? We're supposed to leave promptly at 9:30." She suddenly woke up to the fact that time was marching on.

"Don't worry, Miss Gulliver. We've notified the hotel and the Kingdom Coach Tour representative of the delay. Actually, everyone will have to be questioned until we make sure that there is no question of foul play."

The expression on Claire's face caused the older man to add gently, "What he means is, we have a need to establish Mr. White's death was caused by misadventure, eliminating any question of foul play." He glared at his colleague, as Claire slumped in her chair, the words *foul play* bouncing around in her head.

"The couple, who live in the flat, were out until about 9:30 last night. And, as they didn't hear the body land on their roof, we're assuming he must have fallen before that time. Now you said you talked to him when?"

Claire tried to think but, even though the Inspector referred to Arnie as *the body*, she knew only too well what he was talking about and it made her nauseous. Finally she pulled herself together. "Well, it must have been just before eight, because I wanted to drop the film off and they closed at eight. But where did he and Betty go to dinner? Wasn't she with him?"

The two policemen looked at each other. "What?" Claire said, realizing her voice was getting shrill. "Didn't Arnie have dinner with Betty?"

"Betty apparently had dinner with Warren last night. And what's more, Warren said Arnie knew that, because Warren asked him if he wanted to join them but Arnie said he promised to join you and the others." Inspector Shephard was the older policeman.

"But he told me he couldn't join us as he was dining with Betty. Why would he say...?" Claire looked at them. "You don't think I had...that one of us...?" She just couldn't say it.

He shook his head. "Actually, no. I mean, of course, we did check you out as we did all the members of your group. But apparently you have a fan on the San Francisco Police Force. A Captain Sean Dixon? He not only knows you personally, thinks you're wonderful, but he even suggested you might be of some help to us." The last was said with such disbelief that Claire might have smiled if she hadn't been so upset.

She murmured, "He was buddies with my father. And once I was able to help them, so he's been very appreciative." She really didn't want to discuss the episode.

The Inspector continued gravely, "As of now we have no reason to suspect any of your tour members. In fact, we have no reason to think it was foul play, but we would be remiss if we didn't investigate all possibilities."

"But I don't understand why Arnie would tell me he had a date with Betty and then tell Warren he was going out with us. Why didn't he want anyone to know where he was going?"

Sergeant Makley replied somberly, "Perhaps he was doing something that he didn't want anyone to know about. Had he done this before?"

"Not that I'm aware of. You see it's an *Untour.* So everyone has time to do what they want. No one really checks up on the members. We all know the schedule and we are responsible for being on the bus at the appropriate times." She paused a moment, thinking back. "But now that you mention it, he wasn't at the theatre Wednesday night. Of course, several weren't. We had a little party on the bus and some didn't feel like going out again that night." She realized she was drawing up a list of suspects in her mind and that really disturbed her.

"But, surely it was an accident. I mean he just decided to walk the wall and mis-stepped in the fog. This must happen occasionally. I mean I was up there this morning and even in the daylight it seemed pretty dangerous."

"Actually, we've not had a mishap as long as I've been in these parts. People are pretty careful. Was he despondent? Could it have been a suicide?"

"Oh, no!" She thought a minute trying to give credence to her immediate certainty that Arnie would not have committed suicide. "Why would anybody go to all the trouble and expense to get on this tour just to commit suicide? That doesn't make any sense! I mean, if that's what he wanted, it seems he could have done it back in the States." Then she remembered, paused, and then reluctantly reported, "Well, there was an incident a few nights back."

With their encouragement she continued. "I was walking in the gardens at Hilliary Hall, that's near Castle Combe, when I heard what I thought was an argument. I couldn't hear the words, but I followed the sounds and there was Arnie and Jack Hanford. He's our Kingdom Coach Tours Guide. Anyway, there was something going on but when I interrupted they both denied anything was wrong. But Arnie was upset, I could tell. Jack was cool. He said he was giving Arnie advice about the golf game Arnie had played that afternoon, and Arnie agreed. But I didn't think so. I don't know what it was about because, as I said, I couldn't hear the words. But it seemed as if the tone was very angry. That night Arnie seemed to be having a good time, but I've noticed he stayed out of Jack's way since then."

She looked at them. "But Jack couldn't have had anything to do with it because he was at the Pub when I arrived and I'm sure he was still there when I left. That must have been after ten."

Inspector Shephard nodded his agreement. "Still, it's interesting. And that pub is not far from the wall. Anyone could have disappeared for a few minutes, uh? Maybe we'll have a discussion with Mr. Hanford."

* * *

"Oh, Claire, there you are." Rosa seemed to be waiting for her.

"Where is everyone, Rosa? How are they taking the news?"

"Well, of course, we were all shocked. And, of course, they wouldn't let us leave today." Rosa's manner was stiff, almost cold, as if she was annoyed for all the inconvenience. "I called the Blackpool Guest Cottages and canceled. Fortunately, that city is filled with a convention so they didn't even give me a problem about our canceling. But, of course, we won't be getting our deposit back. It was more of a problem here. But that policeman who was here told them we weren't leaving, so they had to find space. I don't know how, but they did, and we're staying."

Just then Mike and Vern came up. "Claire, this is terrible. How are you doing?"

Mike put his arms around Claire and gave her a hug. This display of sympathy snapped Claire's control and she felt hot tears spring to her eyes. She just shook her head unable to speak.

"Well, everyone has been interviewed. Not that anyone seemed to know anything. I mean, why did he decide to walk on the wall at that time of night?" Vern was clearly disturbed. "Look, why don't you go to your room and have a rest. We talked to the rest of the group, and we've decided to hold a memorial service this afternoon. For Arnie, you know. So we have the parlor reserved for 5:30. Everyone who wants to say something can, and then we'll move on to the pub and do a wake. Okay with you?"

She nodded, heading for the elevator, grateful that she could be alone for a while to think about all this.

* * *

"Fenster, what the hell is going on? I told you no slip-ups, and it looks like we've lost all control."

Fenster was sweating in the cool of Ames' office. "Well, he is such a klutz. I mean, it could have actually been an accident."

"An accident. I thought you said this guy belonged to us?"

"Not really. I mean, he went through training, but he didn't make it to the field. He's always been support. He wasn't supposed to be here." He felt the bile churn in his stomach remembering his embarrassment, then rage when he found out that Arnie White was one of their own alias' being used by Charles Ramsey. Charlie, as he was known, monitored the transmission reports via satellite in California, and noted the same reference to the Springer tour that the Brits had identified. Only Charlie knew about the Lucy Springer *Untour* having seen the announcement in Gulliver's window one evening. But his boss hadn't seen any special value in the information and elected to send the information through the usual channels instead of escalating it as Charlie recommended. Charlie was so certain it was important, he apparently decided to play space cadet and launch himself into what was for him, uncharted space. He took his vacation and got himself on the tour and now he'd gotten himself dead.

It seemed too much of a coincident to be an accident. But with Charlie you never knew. His record with the agency was filled with accidents and mishaps. It was a miracle he had lasted this long, and why he had even thought he could survive in the field was anyone's guess.

This information came right on the heels of the fizzled investigation of Rosa Morino.

Granted, Liz Cooley was very strange. It was hard to have a fifteen-minute conversation with her, without drawing that conclusion. But they took her allegations seriously. How could they not? So their investigators learned that Rosa was well known and respected in her field. She had worked for some very prestigious authors during the past fifteen years. She was not a social person and didn't like long-term assignments. She was good enough to work when she wanted. Before she left her home to work for Lucy Springer, she made all the arrangements for her mail to be forwarded, her house to be watched and left contact numbers with her neighbors. She was a well-established, slightly introverted middle-aged woman who was known in her community. She was not connected to any terrorist group.

Of course, it had been Fenster's duty to report that information to Ames only yesterday. He was beginning to wish the Brits had never told them about the transmissions they intercepted. Yet, there was still a chance that something was happening. There was still a chance this would be their opportunity to nail Guiness. He wouldn't give up on that until he was certain, one way or the other.

* * *

"For Christ's sake, are you crazy?"

"I know what I'm doing!"

"Sure you do. The police are swarming all over the place. What if someone figures it out?" The voice dripped with sarcasm.

"They won't. Why should they? It was an accident." The confidence was unmistakable. "The guy slipped. He was a little strange anyway and no one knows why he was up there in the dark.

"Except me." The voice changed to a ruthlessness that was chilling. "He saw us, you know. After you left I ran into him. He pretended to be surprised and he might have been.

But I couldn't take a chance that he's not the complete nerd he seems to be. He had to go."

"Christ, he was there?"

The line was silent a moment. Then, "How did he know? Will we need to change the next meeting place?" The tone was conciliatory now. Placating. Any witness had to be destroyed. They were in total agreement about that.

"I don't think so but I'll check in tomorrow night at the appropriate number to verify that we're still on schedule."

The anxiety came back to the voice. "They won't cancel the rest of the tour, will they? I mean, they are rather unpredictable. You know we have to keep to the schedule at all costs."

"Don't worry. We won't return early. I'll make sure of that."

"Okay. But remember the whole reason for going with the tour was to remain invisible. And any more accidents will make that impossible. They are getting far too much attention right now."

"I understand. I promise, no more accidents." The click of the receiver emphasized it.

* * *

"Lucy, it's Claire." Claire hated doing this, but it was her responsibility.

"Oh, Claire, how's it going? Didn't you love Conwy?" Suddenly her voice stopped. "What time is it? Shouldn't you be on the road now?"

"Well, something happened."

"Happened? What do you mean something happened?" Lucy's voice rose to a sharper pitch.

"Lucy, I don't know how to tell you this... but we lost Arnie."

"Lost? As in wandered off? How lost..."

Claire's voice was low, trembling, whispering the horror. "No, lost as in he's dead."

She heard the sharp intake of breath and then silence.

"Lucy? Lucy, are you all right?"

"No! No, I'm not all right." Her voice sounded strangled. "Claire, is this some kind of joke, because I can..."

"Lucy, I'm sorry. It's no joke. He apparently went out to walk on the wall here last night. It was very dark and very foggy. You know that wet, slippery kind. Anyway, it appears that he just slipped and fell off the edge. They didn't even find him until this morning."

Claire was panting a little with the effort of getting the story out, and the line hummed silently for a while.

"Oh, my God, Claire. This is awful. How are you doing? How is everyone taking this?"

"Not well. At least I don't feel so well. I haven't seen too many of the others. The police are still questioning everyone."

Lucy's moan came across the line.

"Okay, Claire, can you go through it all again for me? I'm having a little trouble grasping this."

Claire repeated the whole thing. Her visit to the wall this morning, what she saw, what she did. She described her visit to the police station and her conversation with the other tour members. She told her about the plans for a service at the hotel that afternoon and a wake later at the pub down by the wall. And she told her about the inquest in the morning where the cause of death would be decided.

"Cause of death? Do they suspect foul play?" Lucy sounded horrified.

"They said it was to eliminate any possibility of foul play. I don't think they think it's anything but accidental, but they have to be thorough about it. The Inspector told me that as long as he has been here they have never had someone fall off the wall. They just can't believe it happened.

"And frankly, Lucy, I can't believe it either."

"So, you can't leave Conwy?"

"Not for a while. I'm sure that's going to cause Rosa a lot of work. She said that this hotel was in a dither, because we couldn't leave and they had reservations coming in. But they must have worked it out, because we're not leaving. Maybe we can leave tomorrow after the decision is reached. The police will notify Jack."

"Look, Claire, it's too early to decide what to do about the tour. Why don't you see what everyone wants to do when you talk to them this evening? And then we'll talk. Call me after the wake, if you're still sober, and we can brainstorm then."

"Okay. Lucy, I hate to lay this on you, but I think we need to call Arnie's boss. I know the police have contacted his next of kin, but it was his boss who insisted he go on vacation. I think he needs to be told. I was hoping you would do it."

"Oh, Christ, you're right. Oh, the poor man. He will be devastated." Lucy's voice faltered, then rallied. "Okay, you're right. I'll do it."

"Thanks." Claire gave her the police station phone number in case Arnie's boss wanted it.

"Claire, take care. I'm really sorry this happened on your trip."

Claire felt the tears well up again, nodding her head even though Lucy couldn't see her. "I'll call you later."

CHAPTER NINE

"Betty? Come in." A surprised Claire stepped back allowing room for Betty to enter.

Betty looked terrible. Her eyes were swollen. Her face was streaked with makeup mixed with tears. Her hair was tangled and dull. Even one of her nails was jagged.

"I know it's late. I'm sorry..." Betty's sobs didn't allow for more.

Claire led her to the small upholstered chair near the window. And then, not knowing what else to do, she quickly went to fill the electric kettle from the sink in the bathroom. When it was plugged in, its soft pinging signaled its heating cycle was working, she perched awkwardly on her bed waiting for Betty's sobs to subside.

Betty tried to say something but it just came out as a hiccup.

"Wait. We'll have a cup and then you can talk. Okay?"

Betty nodded mutely. Claire assembled the china teapot with tea bags and poured the boiling water over the tea. While it was steeping, she opened and poured two of the little milk containers into the cups, liberally adding two teaspoons of sugar to Betty's cup before filling it with tea.

Betty sipped the tea, making no comment, intermittently dabbing at her nose with a sodden hanky.

Betty had been at the service they held earlier, but Claire hadn't noticed then how upset she obviously was. Maybe because she was too upset herself, taking the blame for Arnie's death? The service had been a comfort, especially as Claire found out every person on the tour somehow felt personally responsible, as if they alone should have, or could have, prevented Arnie's fall.

But Mrs. Maus had put it all in perspective. Perhaps when one aged, one became more reconciled to the fact that death was only a part of living, not just the end. She reminded them all how pleased Arnie was to be included. And she said no matter what reason for Arnie being on the wall, it was not because he wasn't welcome elsewhere. And whatever the cause of his accident, it had occurred while he was doing what he wanted to do.

Claire had been amazed to find out how involved Arnie had become in the group. Everyone had something to say about him; some antidote to share about him. Everyone seemed bewildered by the incident and grieved by his death. But eventually silence fell. There was nothing more to be said. When they moved to a pub, they chose a different one than the one last night. This one held no reminders for any of them. The group speculated on when the police would allow them to leave, discussed the wisdom of canceling the tour versus completing it at this midpoint in the schedule, and the idiosyncrasies of life in general. When Claire finally went to bed, she was emotionally and physically exhausted. And she expected to sleep soundly, but found herself only tossing restlessly until Betty's knock came.

"It was all so stupid."

Claire was fixing a second cup, when Betty just started talking, the sobs no longer choking her, her words coming in a dull monotone.

"There was no reason. And why him? It didn't even make sense.

"We were going to be married in four months. It was all planned. The invitations were addressed just waiting to be mailed." She gulped the hot tea, and then apparently forgetting where she was, she stared off into space.

"You were saying?" Claire prompted her, totally confused, believing Betty was talking about Arnie. How did their relationship develop so quickly?

"I didn't believe them at first. I wouldn't believe them. It was impossible! It was just another business trip. I knew he would be home in a few days. I would just go meet him at the airport like I always did.

"But they insisted he wasn't coming back. His father was bawling like a baby when he talked to me. Still I wouldn't believe him. Finally his sister convinced me. She loved him, too. Maybe as much as I did, but differently, you see. And she believed them. He was dead!

"His father identified him. They wouldn't let me. Not enough left of his head they said. But it was him. His father recognized his clothes, his hands." The agony on Betty's face made Claire flinch.

"I loved his hands, so masculine, yet so gentle. And, the mole on the inside of his left elbow was in the right spot; it was him. I knew it was him but I still couldn't believe it.

"And I couldn't stop crying. The principal said it wasn't good for the children.

"Of course it wasn't. I knew that, but I just couldn't control myself. So I had to take a leave. And then they recommended therapy. I guess it helped. Or maybe it was just the time passing. All those awful, empty days and nights.

"Anyway, my therapist suggested a change and I thought this trip might do it. And it was good. I mean, the people, the places, new things to see and do distracted me. And no one knew anything about Chad.

"Except Arnie." The tears started rolling out of her eyes, but she didn't sob. "He's the only one I told about Chad. He went out of his way to keep me company. He watched out for me. And the other day when we were all drinking on the bus and I started feeling bad again, he took me out for a long walk, just walking with me until I felt better and thought I could sleep. He didn't hit on me. He didn't want anything from me. He was just there when I needed him.

"But, I wasn't there for him. Why did he go up there by himself? I could have gone with him. Anyone would have gone."

Claire had no answers. She was stunned by Betty's sad story. She could only shake her head.

Betty raised her blotched face, looking directly at Claire as she announced, "I want to go home! I know what the others said. I know Arnie wouldn't have wanted to ruin the trip for us. I know he wouldn't. But, it has been ruined!

"I just can't go on pretending it didn't happen. It's all back again. The stupidly, the senselessness of it. Why did it happen? Why? Why?"

The tears were coming faster now, as if the tea she drank had replenished the supply.

"I'm sorry, Claire. I just couldn't wait until morning. I want to go home now, tonight. Right now!"

"But, Betty, you can't go now. I don't even know if the police will release us yet." She tried to keep her voice calm, convincing Betty that her demands were not feasible. "You know they're having some kind of hearing tomorrow. Inspector Shephard told Jack we could probably leave after it was over. I'm sure we can make arrangements then for you to go back to the States."

Betty stubbornly shook her head.

Claire didn't know what to do. "Look, I promise you first thing in the morning I'll get on this and take care of it for you."

Betty just hunched in on herself, grasping the teacup like it was her link to sanity. She looked so miserable Claire almost cried herself. She couldn't fight this kind of grief. She gave in.

"All right. I'll see what I can do. You stay here until I get back." She quickly donned a sweater and pair of pants, choosing to go barefoot rather than look for shoes and socks. She slipped into the dim hall heading for the stairs. This hotel was much simpler to navigate than the first one they stayed in. Thanks to Jack's coach chatter they now all knew that London hotels were frequently formed from clusters of townhouses, built at different times and at different levels. So when they were connected, passageways and stairwells never matched. This hotel, even though it was over one hundred years old, had been built as a hotel. It contained simple halls, normal stairwells and even some ancient elevators, or lifts as the locals said. She went down two floors, hoping Jack was in 111 as she remembered.

She tapped softly at the door, jumping when it swung open before she had even finished. Jack stood there, fully dressed in a dark sweater and jeans. It was hard to decide who was the more surprised.

"I guess you weren't sleeping?" she commented inanely.

He shook his head. "No, hadn't quite got to it as yet." He quirked his eyebrow, asking, "More problems?"

She nodded. "Yes, I need to talk to you."

He hesitated and then stepped back to allow her to enter. But she felt he was less than enthusiastic about it. And no wonder, she thought. They had had nothing but problems.

"I really am sorry to barge in on you like this, but we have a problem with Betty. She's in my room right now. She wants to go home."

He shrugged. "Okay."

"No, she wants to go right now. This minute! Tonight. Now in the middle of the night." Claire saw she finally had Jack's attention, and he was irritated.

"Well, that's impossible. Just tell her we'll take care of it for her tomorrow. I can arrange it in the morning."

"Well, of course I've told her all that. But she is very upset. Very!" Claire watched him carefully. "I think we should try to help her."

She didn't wait for Jack's invitation. She just sat down in his chair and proceeded to explain as best she could about Betty's fiancé, and how seriously upset she was.

"Christ. What next?" Jack frowned and wiped at his brow. "Do you think we should get a doctor in to give her something?"

Claire shook her head. "I suggested something to make her sleep, but she said she had tried that before and it didn't work. It just made things worse when the drugs wore off. I tend to agree with her. I don't like sedatives myself.

"Look, Jack, there's no way we can get her out of here tonight! I know that. But I thought if you could call and make the arrangements, I could go and help her get packed. By then it will be early morning. We can contact Inspector Shephard for permission for her to leave, and then maybe we can have her on the first train out. She doesn't want to see anyone else in our group. She doesn't want them to know. She doesn't want to feel like she needs to explain."

Claire couldn't tell what he was thinking. His face gave no clue, so she just waited. Suddenly she wondered if it was safe to leave Betty alone in her room for this long. As soon as that thought hit her she jumped up, heading for the door.

"Let's go up to my room. Betty's there. I don't think she should be alone while she's this upset. We can talk about it there. Okay?"

She paused only long enough to see his curt nod, her anxiety spreading to Jack, and he followed her back through the dim corridors and up the stairs, this time to her own room. She was very relieved to see Betty, just as she left her, except the tears were down to a trickle now.

Jack pushed past her and went to kneel in front of Betty taking both of her hands, teacup and all, in his own. He spoke to her in such a low voice Claire couldn't hear what he said. Whatever it was, it seemed to offer comfort to Betty. When he got up, he handed the teacup to Claire and said, "All right. I'll go get on the phone. You and Betty get her stuff together. Call me when you're ready."

When Claire first saw Betty's room, she didn't believe they could get it all together and packed in time for her to leave in the morning. She remembered as a teenager going over to her friend's home and seeing her room like this, clothes, books, and papers, everywhere. It was hard for the orderly Claire to believe someone, who looked as well turned out as Betty, could emerge from chaos such as this. But two hours later, Betty showered and dressed, was working miracles on her hair, while Claire rounded up the last of the clothes that would have to be stuffed in the already overflowing suitcase.

Jack had rung twice, once to get Betty's credit card information for the train fare and once to ask Claire if she thought Betty would be able to cope with changing trains three times.

"Ready?" Jack was at the door.

"I thought we were going to call you?"

"We don't have time. Let's get going."

Betty was leaning on the suitcase, pushing escaping items back into the interior, while forcing it to close with the practice of experience.

Claire noticed Jack's expression and looked down realizing that she wasn't dressed. She promised to meet them in the lobby in five minutes and raced off to her own room, leaving Jack to help Betty get her bag locked and downstairs.

"Jack, did you call Inspector Shephard?" Her voice was hushed when she joined them in the deserted lobby.

Jack shook his head. "We're going to stop over there. That way they'll have to deal with us." He herded them out the door and into a waiting taxi.

Jack was right. The sleepy officer on duty didn't want to get involved in such a complex situation so close to the end of his shift. He tried to convince them they would have to come back at a later time. But failing that strategy, he finally called Inspector Shephard at home. Claire didn't hear what the sleepy Inspector said to Jack. He must have been unhappy about having his sleep disturbed, but Jack finally convinced him to allow Betty to leave. They then left immediately for Llandudno where a train would take her to Chester. From there Betty would travel to Birmingham and change to a train headed for London. Jack had arranged for one of Kingdom Coach Tours representatives to meet her at the London station and transport her to Heathrow. There he would see her onto the plane. Jack assured Betty that it was the least they could do to try to make up for the mishaps on this tour which caused her so much distress.

Claire was impressed. It was a very thoughtful thing for the company to do, and she resolved to make sure that she let them know how she appreciated their courtesy. After seeing all the care taken she felt much better about Betty traveling clear across the country to make the flight that Jack had scheduled.

* * *

"Lucy, were you able to contact Arnie's boss?"

"Yes, finally. I had to leave a message and he called me back. He already knew about Arnie, thank God. I wasn't looking forward to being the bearer of that news. He said he appreciated my call, but I must say he was rather abrupt. But then he must have been upset and some people just handle it that way."

"Well, when I get home I'll call him and tell him how much Arnie was liked by the group, and about the wake." She paused a moment, then changed the subject.

"The inquest or inquiry, or whatever they call it, is over and they ruled Arnie's death 'misadventure'.

"It seems so inadequate to explain away someone's death that way," she mused.

"Oh, Claire, I'm so sorry. I'm sorry for poor Arnie, even though I barely knew the man. And I'm especially sorry you've had to go through all this. I expected you to have such a good time."

Claire continued, "Apparently Arnie just used poor judgment in going up there. And we'll never know why. Maybe he just wanted to be alone for a while. After all, traveling with twenty some people doesn't give anyone much quiet time, and I think he was used to being alone."

"Claire," Lucy's voice was firm, "you just keep telling yourself this wasn't your fault. I know you, and just because you allowed him to join the trip doesn't make you responsible. It was just one of those things."

"I know that. I mean, my mind follows the logic, but I still feel like something was there I didn't see, or there was something I could have done. It turned out that I was the last one to have spoken to him, but I didn't sense anything. I didn't have a clue."

"You don't run the world. So stop it!" Lucy told her emphatically. Then, "What have you decided about Hopsvale Farms?"

"We're taking your suggestion, of course. Rosa told us how it would work, after she talked to you this morning, and we all agree with you. We're leaving here in about an hour and we can drive straight through, stay at Hopsvale Farms tonight and pick up the tour as scheduled tomorrow." Everyone was pleased to be back on the schedule with so little fuss. Then she remembered, "Oh, Lucy, I forgot to tell you. Betty Brown is on her way back."

"Not another problem?"

"Not exactly. Remember how private she was, never saying much about herself? We thought she was escaping from a soured romance, remember? Well it turns out her fiancé was murdered several months ago when he was on a business trip. It was a random shooting from a passing car outside his hotel. She hasn't been able to get over it and signed up for this trip on the advice of her therapist.

"She's taking Arnie's accident very badly. She insisted on going home.

"Don't worry though. Jack took care of all the arrangements and Kingdom Coach Tours is meeting her train and will see she gets on the plane. Her parents will pick her up in San Francisco. You don't have to do anything, and when I get back I'll give her a call. Maybe we can both go visit her. But meanwhile, I just told the others that she decided to go back. She can't bear for anyone to know about her loss. I guess it's her protection somehow."

"Oh, no. Poor Claire. I can't believe what I got you into. I've never had a trip with any of these problems and here you are on your first. Please don't think traveling is always like this. Trust me, it's never like this!"

"Don't worry, Lucy. The tour is going well and everyone is delighted with it, from what I'm hearing. I think the travel bug has bitten us all. I expect we can complete these last few days with the group intact and with no more problems.

"Now you take care of yourself, and that leg, and I'll call you again in a couple of days."

* * *

By the time Claire realized she could no longer see the lambs cavorting in the pasture, it was too late. Darkness had come. Total blackness—the only spots of light were far in the distance. She assumed they were the farm buildings where they were staying.

She clutched the fence she had been leaning on, eyes straining to identify the path, anything that would give her an idea about how to get back. There were no streetlamps, no lighted windows and no flashing neon signs.

She felt a rush of panic. Darkness did this. It brought it all back, that total blackness, the confusion, the terror.

Why hadn't she considered this when she impulsively turned up the path to the pastures after dinner. All she had been thinking about was getting some fresh air and looking at the lambs Teri described so enthusiastically. It had never occurred to her it would get so dark.

Then a movement behind her made her jump. Her heart beat painfully, knocking so hard she could barely force the words out. "Who's there?"

"It's only me. Are you ready to go back?" A column of light sprang from the flashlight in his hand.

"Oh, Jack, you scared me." She could hear the quiver in her voice and she would have been angry with him for sneaking up on her, if she hadn't been so grateful he was there.

"I didn't want to disturb you. You seemed lost in thought so I just waited." He was beside her now. She could feel the comforting nearness of him.

"When I saw you heading up the path after dinner, I assumed you hadn't brought your torch." She heard the smile in his voice. "You city folks never know how to act in the country."

She laughed. "Guilty. I had a few bad moments there when I realized there were no streetlamps or neon signs to light the way for me."

"I was surprised to see you head up here. I would have thought you'd be off to bed early after last night." He casually slipped his arm around her waist directing her down the path behind the column of light.

"I didn't think I'd have much success in sleeping. And after listening to Teri describe how they watched the farmers move the sheep this afternoon, I thought a little commune with nature might relax me."

"Did it?"

She laughed. "It did, until I thought I would probably have to sleep leaning against that fence. Thanks again for rescuing me."

"All part of the service."

They followed the light for a while, avoiding the holes and obstructions it revealed in the path.

"He didn't even want to go on vacation, you know." Her voice was low, conveying her thoughts almost unconsciously. "He came at the last minute. His boss was forcing him to take vacation because of the doctor's warning. His boss said he was too valuable to lose." She was dangerously close to tears, but she had to finish what was haunting her.

"And now he's gone. A stupid missed step they said." Her words hung there. The only response from Jack was a tightening of his arm, pulling her comfortingly closer to him.

The stars were now so dense they gave off a soft glow. The night sounds were reassuring: the panicked bleat of a lamb and the answer from its mother, frogs or crickets or something chirping from the fields they passed, and a mysterious rustling of leaves at the edge of the path.

They passed some of the outbuildings now. A dimly lit path was just ahead. At her door Jack hugged her to him tightly. She felt the tension running out of her body. He kissed her lightly on the forehead and with a "Sleep well, Claire," he left her and followed his light back towards the main house.

Claire wondered for a minute before sinking into a deep sleep how he felt about Arnie's death. He hadn't said, and she didn't ask.

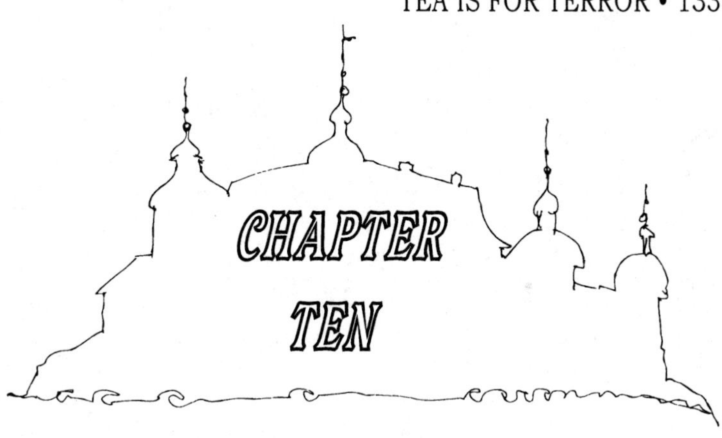

CHAPTER TEN

Hopsdale Farms Slaidburn, Yorkshire Day 10--Sunday Dear Mrs. B, We stayed last night at this wonderful farm. I was up with the dawn to get the most enjoyment from our too short stay. I walked down to the village. It's so beautiful it doesn't seem like it can be real. All the buildings, and there are not many, are built out of gray stone. Everything is just the way it was built hundreds of years ago except for an occasional car or two. There was even a family that drove a pony cart into church this morning. I have so much to tell you when I get back. Love, Claire	Mrs. B C/o Gulliver's 714 Elm Avenue Bayside, CA 94403 U.S.A AIR MAIL

* * *

"All right folks, where are we?"

"How Wath," they responded, gathering their things and filing off the coach to explore the tiny village spread on either side of the street going up the side of the steep hill.

"I love *Jane Eyre*. I think I've read it at least twenty times. And the movies! Did you see Joan Fontaine playing Jane? I swear she was Jane. But the English version with George C. Scott playing Mr. Rochester still makes my heart flutter."

Claire laughed at Alice's enthusiasm. "I guess I just wasn't the romantic you were, but I did like *Jane Eyre*. I just couldn't get through *Wuthering Heights*. And the other sister wrote books too. Can you imagine all that talent coming out of this little house?"

Claire thought the tiny rooms were hardly as big as a closet in today's California houses. Charlotte's room overlooked the gloomy graveyard of the church—so much better to inspire the budding author. The day was perfect for visiting the birth site of the gothic romance novel. Gray clouds hung low and the wind moaned through the churchyard. A hint of winter, long past, helped them imagine the bleakness of the sisters' lives, no excitement, no prospects of any kind except their brother staggering home after a long hard day at the local pub. The house, museum really, was filled with letters, pages of the manuscripts and memorabilia from the family's life. Interesting as it was, it was still a relief to get out of doors and wander up the street looking in the windows of the little shops.

"Maybe we should just find the local and have a couple before the coach leaves."

"Not yet. Let's go in this shop. I promised Mrs. B a sweater, and I think she'd be thrilled if it came from How Wath."

Alice laughed at her careful pronunciation of the tricky Haworth as she followed her into the little shop and joined in the process of picking just the right cardigan for Mrs. B. Teri and Shar saw them as they passed and came in to see what was attracting them. They were still examining each of the exquisite hand-knit sweaters when Claire, her final selection made, headed down the street with Alice to an inviting looking pub they noticed on the way up.

"Do you think this trip is going to turn us into one of those beer guzzling middle-aged women who hang out in the local bars? I swear I'm getting a real taste for this stuff."

"Not to worry. It's hard finding lukewarm beer in the States. Besides, I don't know about you but I never have time for lunch, say nothing about hanging out drinking beer.

Alice accepted this. "You're right. It wouldn't taste the same surrounded by plastic stools and a jukebox."

Claire sank down in a seat near the fire, looking around at the pub, the duplicate of countless others they had visited on their trip. Each pub, with different names and at various locations, was always the same, the hub of the neighborhood, and the gathering place of the locals.

Tom, John and Mike were playing darts, but Vern picked up his pint and came over to join Claire and Alice by the fire inquiring, "Where is everyone?"

"We saw Teri and Shar in one of the shops and the Martinez's were with Joe and Mrs. Maus up in the cemetery when we came out from the Bronte's house." Alice shrugged. "I haven't seen the rest."

"It's such a small village you'd think we'd be very obvious."

"Well, Jack took Warren, Kim and Annie somewhere. I heard the girls talking about it in the bus."

Claire was glad the dimness in the pub hid the blush heating her cheeks at the mention of Jack. Only a few days ago he was annoying her no end. Now, just because he had been the gallant last night, she was acting like those poor Bronte sisters had, trapped in a harsh and barren life, looking to their imaginations for romance.

"Vern, didn't you go up to the Bronte's house? Isn't this your kind of thing?" she inquired purposely shifting her thoughts.

"It is, and I did. I just came in a little before you did. Mike was more interested in darts, so he stayed here with the guys. I think he's practicing to challenge Glenda again."

They all laughed. Since Mike's first humiliation at the dartboard, he had challenged Glenda at every opportunity only to lose bigger stakes each time. Of course, Mike was taking a good deal of ribbing over this ongoing match, but so far he hadn't seemed able to give it up. However, he had heeded Alex's warning and stayed away from the billiards table. In fact, the few times Glenda had innocently asked if anyone wanted to play pool with her, everyone begged off. Poor Glenda. She didn't know her loving husband had warned them off.

Shar poked her head in the door, gestured to her watch and withdrew. Alice drained the last of her glass, but Claire and Vern gave up, leaving half-filled glasses as they headed for the door. The guys followed. Tom and John wondered out loud where Joan and Mary were. Mike insisted he was so far ahead at darts when they had been interrupted, they shouldn't even think they could have won.

Back on the bus, Jack had distributed the little boxes containing sandwiches, crisps and fruit. Claire decided to use this time to catch up with Rosa. She gathered up her lunch and moved to the back, joining Rosa without an invitation. Rosa preferred her privacy and usually Claire humored her, but now she wanted to make sure Rosa had been able to contact the rest of the hotels on the agenda and cancel Betty's room. She understood it was too short notice to cancel Hopsdale Farms in time for a refund, but she knew Rosa was annoyed about not being in the loop about the decision to send Betty home, and Claire didn't want her to retaliate by not canceling the rest of Betty's booked rooms in a timely manner.

Actually, everyone was concerned about Betty's sudden disappearance. But after Jack and Claire explained, they all seemed to accept that Betty just didn't want to go on. So Rosa's attitude was even more annoying.

Rosa seemed personally affronted that Betty left, which made Claire all the more determined not to explain the whole situation to her. She didn't think Rosa would have any sympathy for Betty's plight, so she refused to tell her about it. But, since Rosa was here as a favor for Lucy, Claire would do whatever she could to help her accomplish her tasks.

"Rosa, I know you have a lot of work to do in York. Could I be of any help in checking some of the data about prices and hours of the museums or attractions?"

Rosa seemed surprised at Claire's offer and didn't respond at once. Claire waited, watching her face. She still had no idea how old Rosa was. Her inky black hair was a color which usually came from a bottle. She applied her makeup heavily, rimmed her eyes with black liner and thick mascara as was used in the sixties. And the bright red mouth was painted according to her taste regardless of her lip lines. She always wore either a scarf or a high-necked sweater, which Claire assumed was to disguise the horrid chicken neck that so often revealed a woman's advancing years. Rosa looked hard and brittle—the complete opposite of what Claire had imagined when Lucy first told her about Rosa coming to assist her. Then she had imagined a graying blonde, with a little middle-age spread, prone to simpering giggles, and speaking with a soft southern accent. She couldn't have been more wrong.

Finally she got a response. "That's nice of you, Claire. But really, I have it under control. I'll get it all done and still have time for myself."

Rosa was confident. Her mouth stretched into a grimace that Claire assumed was a smile. But she repeated her offer. "Well, I know missing Blackpool, and then all the changes in arrangements, has added to your tasks. So I just wanted you to know I'd be happy to help."

Rosa paused a moment. "That's really very kind. I appreciate your offer. And if I need help, don't worry, I'll come to you. And Claire," she paused momentarily and then looked away while she continued, "I'm sorry about how I acted about Betty. After all, if she decided to go back, if all of them decided to go back, it really doesn't make any difference to my job here. I'd just have to go on for Mrs. Springer. So I apologize if I was rude. I was just overly concerned that something else had happened."

"Don't worry about it. I know this trip has been difficult for you. Not only have you had to verify all Lucy's information, but you've had to adjust the reservations as we go. First Liz, then Arnie, and now Betty." Claire was now comforting Rosa, apologizing to her instead of being firm with her as she planned. "But we only have four more days. Surely we won't have any more incidents."

She moved back to her own seat not convinced that she had achieved anything for her efforts. But, she told herself, admitting her pettiness, she still hadn't relieved Rosa's curiosity over Betty's departure.

* * *

"This has been the trip from Hell. What's the story on this Betty Brown?"

"It all checks out. We had someone with her all the way back. No contacts, no suspicious actions. We even put someone on the plane next to her, so we'll get that report soon after they land." Fenster was disgusted. Nothing on this tour was going right.

"The verdict was *Misadventure.* What's so irritating is that I believe it was. The more I learn about Charles Ramsey, the more I think that he just fell off that damn wall. His file is filled with blunders and mistakes. I'm surprised they kept him on, but this episode is unbelievable. Talk about bad timing.

"And it's quiet out there. No one has heard anything. None of the listening posts have anything. None of the regulars have anything to say. It's too quiet. I don't like it. Maybe this thing with Charlie spooked Guiness. Maybe he called it off."

Ames didn't answer, just examined the report once again, studying the details of Charles (Charlie) Ramsey's career. "Well, it's the best lead we've had in a long time. If something is going down, if Guiness is still out there, we're going to be ready. We'll keep with it to the end.

"But, I suspect you're right. If it was scheduled, it may have been called off. Charles may have blown the whole thing. Stupid schmuck!"

They looked at each other a moment, the unkind epithet for their colleague echoing harshly through the room.

Ames shook his head in sorrow and turned his attention to his putter while Fenster let himself out quietly.

* * *

The morning's gloom that enveloped Haworth had broken up, allowing short periods of dazzling afternoon sun to spotlight the dramatic ruins of Bolton Abbey which sat in a large meadow at the bend of the River Wharfe. Claire was content to wander, awed at the size of this Abbey built in the twelfth century and later abandoned. The age and grandeur seemed so acceptable in England, and at home the only thing to compare was some of the weathered Indian dwellings hanging on the cliffs in Arizona and New Mexico. She stood on the bridge watching some of the tour members crossing the river further down on big square steppingstones.

"Hey, Claire, head over this way with Jack and give me a little action."

Claire joined Jack and Joe on the bridge and walked towards Tom's video camera, waving and pointing out things about the view.

"So, do you like our ruins?"

"I can't tell you how much. We have nothing like this in the States. And if we did, someone would make it into a tourist attraction that would cost money."

"Actually, that's happened here in many places. Some of the gentry actually built houses from the stones, some on top of old ruins. Some of the large estates were built to take advantage of the view of picturesque ruins. Your Lucy did well in picking this site. I prefer Fountains Abbey myself, but it's a little out of the way for this tour."

Then as Joe wandered away to join the Mohney's, Jack continued in a lower tone. "Betty got home all right. I called my office this morning and they confirmed it."

Claire sighed, feeling a weight removed from her shoulders. "I've been wondering. Thanks for letting me know."

"Right. Well, now only a few days left, and hopefully you can just enjoy them. I know you'll like York and I'm pretty interested in this place we're going in Sheffield. I've never been there.

"I'm not sure I'll convince you, but this has been a very unusual trip. I've never had one that had any problem more serious than one of the group getting mugged or a few having stomach problems. You really have had more than your share. But I have so admired your ability to cope with everything that I'm finally ready to forgive you for knocking me down the stairs that first morning."

Claire was surprised at his stiff formal words and then she started laughing as he meant her to. They both remembered how hostile they had been, neither having any idea they would be traveling together.

"Look, Claire, why don't I take you out to dinner tomorrow night? I know a charming little place in York and we can just enjoy ourselves and forget about the rest of the group?" He waited, eyebrow crooked.

"Out to dinner?"

He nodded. "People do, you know."

She laughed. "I guess I'd forgotten. Sure, that sounds like fun. What time shall I meet you?"

"Eight o'clock, in the lobby. And don't forget, just the two of us. We're leaving responsibility behind for the entire evening."

"I'll look forward to it."

* * *

"OK, we're back on schedule. Everyone is checked in and accounted for. No new surprises or disappearances."

"Did you find out why Betty left?"

"No, but I don't think it will have any impact on us. No one knows much, and those that might aren't saying. I think it was something personal."

"So you're confident everything is going forward as scheduled."

"I said, didn't I?" The voice sounded irritated. "You just take care of that camera as we decided. We don't want any film around that may have our faces on it.

"Are you sure this is the only one to worry about?"

"Yes, they're the only ones not going back with the group. They decided to spend four more days in London before returning. Thankfully, not many of them were willing to be that adventurous, or you'd have a real problem."

"And you're sure Betty didn't have pictures?"

"I told you, I never saw her pointing a camera. And as I had no warning that she was leaving, there wasn't any time

to take precautions. There's not much we can do about it right now. Just take care of the video camera."

"All right, just checking. I'll do it tomorrow."

"Are you awake?"

Lucy sounded sleepy. "Awake, yes. Up? No. What time is it anyway?"

"Well, it's about cocktail time here, so you should be up," Claire teased her.

"Says you. I like to have my paper and coffee in bed before facing the day. Except when I'm traveling, of course." Lucy's haughty tone suddenly turned sharp with anxiety. "So how is it going? I hope you're not calling with more bad news."

"No, nothing like that. Jack told me Betty landed safely, so we can let her family and her therapist worry about her now."

Then her voice perked up and the enthusiasm came across the line loud and clear. "I loved the farm. It was just what we all needed after all the stress at Conwy. I'd like to go back and spend a few days there sometime."

"Isn't the food good? Mrs. Sinclair makes the most delightful lamb roast I've ever had. That rosemary crust is—"

"Lucy, how could you?" Claire was horrified.

"What? What...?"

"How could you eat lamb? There? Have you no heart?"

"Claire, they raise them to eat." Lucy's voice turned droll. "I suppose I'll have to explain about the Easter bunny next."

Claire laughed. "Okay, I know they're going to be eaten. Actually I love lamb, but I just couldn't eat it and then look those little lambs in the face." She explained righteously, "I had Dover Sole. Mr. Sinclair recommended it. He said you couldn't get real Dover Sole outside of England, no matter what other places called it. So I took his advice, albeit hesitantly because of my experience with the Plaice, which everyone here thinks is such a wonderful fish. But happily, the sole was wonderful."

"You didn't like the Plaice?"

"Ugh, no. It was mealy and soft and tasted funny. And I tried it at two different places, because I was so convinced that it must be good. I just don't like it.

"Anyway, I was telling you about the farm. Everyone was talking during dinner about moving the sheep to another pasture, so I decided to take a walk up there for some fresh air before going to bed. You know, kind of see it for myself.

"It was lovely. I've seen lambs before, but in fields along the road. I didn't know that they just leap up in the air for no reason, and they chase each other, playing like children.

"Anyway, before I knew it, it was dark. I mean completely black! And, of course, I didn't think to bring a light with me."

"Oh, no, what did you do?"

"Well, first I panicked; then I was rescued."

"Rescued. You're kidding? Just like in the movies?"

"Yep, Jack saw me start out and suspected I was too stupid to take a light. So he did and followed me. I was pretty glad to see him, I can tell you that."

"Oooh. Do I detect a little softening toward the roguish Jack?" Lucy had listened to her complaints about the irritating Jack and knew she could get away with a little teasing.

"I guess he's not as bad as I first thought," Claire admitted grudgingly. "I'll find out more tomorrow night. He's taking me out to dinner."

"A date? Ah, wait. I'm getting a message. Yes, yes, I see it. A touch of romance is finally going to save this trip for you?"

"Very funny. Don't get that writer's imagination of yours in an uproar. This is real life. We're going to dinner and in three more days I'm getting on a plane and flying to the other side of the world. If by some remote chance there is a touch of romance, it will be very brief and very tepid.

"And remember, we have eighteen chaperons.

"But I think it will be fun to learn a little more about him and what life is really like in Britain."

"Of course, dear. It's just a bit of cultural research..." and Lucy laughed until Claire hung up.

* * *

"Move to the right a little, Mike. Alice, you too. Vern face the Minster." Claire, finally satisfied with the view of her group standing on the wall near Petergate with the Minster behind them, snapped the picture.

It wasn't discussed, but the group broke into segments for their walks on the ancient wall of York. The incident at

Conwy was still fresh in all of their hearts and no one was walking that wall by themselves. Claire and Alice had joined Mike and Vern to trek the whole way around right after breakfast. It allowed them an amazing view of the bustling medieval town. And Lucy was right. It was totally different than Conwy. York was a tourist Mecca. The tiny streets twisted through the labyrinth of the town. Ancient buildings hung crookedly over the streets, leaning unevenly but very solidly, wedged together in compact rows. Not likely any of them would be demolished by the wrecker's ball. If one went, they would all topple. And of course, they were now housing picturesque shops, very attractive to the tourists, who wanted to shop and eat and sip coffee and tea and most of all take endless pictures.

After finishing their walk on the wall, Alice and Claire headed back to the street market they spotted earlier. Alice had visited the weekly market in Hay-on-Wye, but Claire had been closeted in the bookstores. This market wasn't like the crafts fairs they attended in the States, or the Camden Market they visited in London. This weekly market set up in a different town each day of the week. Here they sold everything from meats and foodstuffs to clothes, house wares and even pets. The stalls offered a wide profusion of fruits and vegetables even in this remote northern part of England. And many of the shops were specially equipped RV's—one was a rolling butcher shop, one a cheese shop and even one was a candy shop.

The tourists were in minority as the locals crowded in to do their weekly shopping, haggling furiously with their favorite vendors. And should the tired shoppers need sustenance the food stalls offered a variety of food and drink to sustain them. The whole scene was colorful and lively. Claire wondered what it would be like to live this way, to make the time in your schedule to attend the market day in your area or to go without until the next one.

She succumbed at one stall offering knitting wool. Her mother was an avid knitter and would love the luxurious skein Claire bought from a woman who raised the sheep, prepared the wool and spun it into a lush combination of mohair and wool. She prayed she would be able to compress it enough to get it into her suitcase.

They dropped their purchases back at the hotel, then ducked into a pub in one of the crooked buildings hanging over the little lane called *Shambles* for a pint in lieu of lunch. They had nibbled their way through the market and weren't ready for a real lunch. Afterwards they wanted to visit the famous Minster. It was hard to believe anything so elegant, complex and huge could have been built in the tenth century. Shar and Teri were there and convinced them to see the Viking Exhibit with them. It took a while as there was a long line and Claire thought the boats sailing deep underground through Viking villages was not up to Disney quality, but it was interesting enough. By then they were all ready for tea and scones at a tiny shop. Claire begged off joining them to shop until they dropped, she knew how Shar was, she examined everything in detail; she could shop for hours. Claire admitted she was going back to the hotel for a needed rest and privately she had decided on a relaxing bath before meeting Jack.

York was too small to get lost in. Still the area was not one Claire had been in before. The sky had turned very dark and now it was threatening rain making the tiny twisting streets confusing. She knew from her little map she was headed in the right direction but, none-the-less, she was pleased when she saw the Pedersons and the Sorinis ahead. Claire quickened her step to catch up with them.

Tom dropped back to film the street and swung the camera around catching Claire in the lens. He lowered the camera and waved. “Come on, Claire. This will be a great street scene.

“It’s too dark, Tom. You won’t get anything with all these shadows.”

Tom ignored his wife’s comments. He considered himself a burgeoning Spielberg. “You go on with John and Mary and, when Claire passes, I can swing around and get you all.”

Joan just shrugged, grinning at Claire, and went on down the street after the Pedersons.

Claire felt a little self-conscious, the eye of the camera following her relentlessly. Later, she wasn’t even sure she heard the pounding footsteps coming up behind her. But she must have, because she instinctively pulled her backpack hanging on one shoulder to the front, clutching it protectively with both hands. When the bodies hurdled by her, one of them crashed against her so she stumbled, almost falling. Tom wasn’t so lucky. He didn’t let go of the camera fast enough, or his camera bag, which had been twisted around his arm.

Claire yelled and the others ran back hollering. It was no use. The camera, the bag and the thugs were gone down a dark alley cut between two of the ancient buildings. And Tom was on the ground.

“Tom, oh, Tom. Are you hurt?” Joan was down beside him, checking him over.

"Those bastards. Did you see that? They took my new camera." Tom's voice was thick with pain or rage, maybe both.

John veered toward the little alley as if to chase them down, but Mary was more clearheaded. "John, don't be crazy. There could be others. They could be waiting for you. Come back."

John returned with a sheepish look. "Is he hurt? Tom, did they hurt you? Should we call an ambulance? Or should I just get a cab so we can take Tom straight to the hospital."

Tom shook his head. "No, get the police. There may be a chance of getting my stuff back if they catch them fast enough. I didn't even get a look at them. Did you, Claire?"

Claire shook her head. "Only from the back, not enough to identify them."

"Well, if we get the camera, we'll have them. I got a good picture of them running right at me."

"There's a Pub up the way a bit. Mary and I can go up there and see if they can call the police for us," John offered, wanting to do something, shocked at this sudden attack on his friend.

"Yah, go on, John. See if you can get the police. I'm just going to sit here for a few minutes and catch my breath. I'm getting too old to jump right up after being dumped on my butt."

John and Mary hurried off, and Joan hunkered down beside Tom examining him closely as a mother does a child, looking at the bruises quickly forming around his eye and cheek where the struggle for the camera had done the most apparent damage.

Claire kept an eye on the street. The shadows were deepening and she didn't want them to be surprised a second time. She was relieved to catch sight of John and Mary returning, and then from the other direction two bobbies on bicycles appeared.

The rather benign appearance of the police in their picturesque helmets and on the harmless bicycles was deceiving. They were very professional in their interview, taking what appeared to be copious notes and then bundling them in a cab directed to the local hospital. The bobbies didn't give Tom much hope for recovering his camera and bag, reminding them that recovery in York would be as likely as it probably was in San Francisco.

"But York is a small town, so we may find it. Still someone will stop by your hotel in the morning to give you an update before you leave. We are sorry this happened. We don't like our tourists having a problem in Yorkshire. We'll do our best."

It was a relief to let the taxi driver find his way through the twisted streets to the hospital. And then in the emergency ward, there was a long wait for Tom's name to be called.

"I can't believe it's all gone," Tom complained. "I had such a wonderful record of the whole trip. I was going to edit it down and show it to everyone at a reunion. Now I have nothing.

"I hope those bastards enjoy the film," he groused.

By the time he was led away, the bruise and cut over his eye was not the worst of his injuries. His hand and wrist had swollen to twice its normal size and turned an ugly purple color. They were all hoping it wasn't broken.

John had found the vending machines and had eaten a sandwich of thick, stale roll with a paper-thin slice of ham, three packages of crisps and uncounted cups of tepid tea. He settled on the tea after throwing out the vile brew he swore was labeled coffee. Mary had a few of his crisps and Claire had a cup of the tea while she thumbed through the assortment of papers and magazines left on the chairs.

Tom looked pale when he and Joan reappeared, making the bruises on his cheek and eye around the small bandage look even darker than they had.

“Thanks for waiting. Just a sprain.” He held up his hand, now wrapped with an elastic bandage.

They all headed for the door and the cabstand. “Does anyone want to get something to eat or a drink?” John asked glancing at his watch.

“Tom can’t. The doctor gave him a shot and some pills. He’s supposed to go to bed and get some rest.”

Claire shook her head. She didn’t feel like eating. She glanced at her watch and saw it was almost ten. Now she remembered with dismay she was supposed to have had dinner with Jack at eight.

At the hotel they all split up, John and Mary heading for a pub up the street, the Sorinis heading for their room. When Claire picked up her key, she asked if Jack was in his room. The clerk shook his head. His key was in the box indicating he was out. Claire asked for a piece of paper and an envelope and scribbled a short apology, which she left with the clerk to give him when he picked up his key.

* * *

It was very early when she woke. She saw the note Jack pushed under her door, and she called his room as he instructed her to do.

"God, what time is it?" he growled into the receiver without even a greeting.

"You told me to call." Claire was embarrassed.

That seemed to wake him up. "Right, right. Your note didn't tell me much, and it was too late when I got back to knock on doors. What happened?"

"It's a long story, and I'm hardly awake yet. Why don't I get sorted out here and meet you downstairs in about a half hour. Then we can talk and eat at the same time."

"Can't."

"Can't?"

"They don't start serving until seven."

"Oh, well we can have coffee while we wait. They might take pity on us." Claire assumed the grunt was his agreement and she quickly organized her things and got dressed.

When Claire entered the dining room Jack had already claimed a table for two in the back corner, ensuring them some privacy even when the others started to arrive.

"Coffee or tea?" He smiled smugly indicating the two pots on the table. "Toast is on the way and they'll take our order then."

"Tea. I've had too many nasty surprises when I ordered coffee."

Jack nodded. "And it's so much better than it used to be. But some places still persist in making their coffee the way Americans make tea. They just dunk a coffee bag in hot water." He added drolly, "It's enough to make you cautious."

Claire had to laugh remembering Lucy's complaints about ordering tea in restaurants at home, always instructing the waitress to bring her *boiling* water, not hot water.

The toast arrived. Claire impressed Jack with the size of the breakfast she ordered and helped herself to cold cereal. After she finished the cereal she proceeded to explain to Jack what had occurred.

"So, I didn't really forget our date. I mean, that's why I headed back early. It's just that when everything started to happen, that's when I forgot."

"Well, I feel better. I thought I was losing it. I mean, at first I was concerned and then I thought maybe you had decided to do something else."

"I am sorry, Jack. I wouldn't have stood you up without saying something. Truly, I was looking forward to our little escape."

Jack nodded. "Forget it. I'm just sorry it happened."

When their breakfast arrived Claire was busy for a while. Then as her need for food abated she filled her cup with more tea and frowned at Jack. "I think I'm getting a little paranoid, but I'm really concerned with all the problems we've had on this trip."

Jack's quizzical look encouraged her.

"Look, before we even left, Lucy broke her leg. Then Liz had an accident. I'm sure it really was an accident in spite of Liz insisting Rosa did it on purpose. And Arnie. That was so bizarre it's still hard to even think about it. Then Betty. But that was really a result of Arnie's accident. I wonder how many times someone just leaves a tour, and in the middle of the night?"

Jack shook his head.

"Then this thing about Tom. I mean, why him? The town is full of tourists." She paused to think.

"The policemen said the kids probably saw his camera and followed him until they saw the opportunity to take it." She shuddered. "I had been going down that street by myself, feeling spooky, wondering why I went that way. Then I saw the Sorinis and the Pedersons.

"I was so relieved to see them I didn't care about starring in his video. And then, wham. It was gone, Tom was on the ground and the kids had disappeared."

She saw Jack's face. "I know." She held up her hand. "I know. I shouldn't be walking in dark lonely places by myself."

"So? What's your point?" Even though Jack's expression was neutral, Claire could sense a tension in him that indicated some interest in her opinion.

"I don't know. That's the point. It's all too weird. Why this tour? Why so many incidences? Someone wants us to go home? Someone is a crazy?" She shrugged; making sense of it was hopeless. "But, I can't help feeling something isn't right. I feel like I'm missing something."

"Maybe you're looking at this the wrong way. Maybe it was a good thing Liz had to return. No, I don't mean about her accident or her pain. But she was a pain to everyone else, so the tour was definitely better after she left. There was an obvious easing of tension, so, maybe that wasn't a bad thing. Perhaps that was a good thing."

Claire thought about it a moment, nodding. What he said was true.

"I have to admit losing Arnie was bad. Very bad! One of the other tour guides had a women die of a heart attack on one of his trips, and it was a real shocker. But that's the only other time my company has lost someone.

"Arnie was a nice guy but he was a bit clumsy. The police think it was simply an accident. And just knowing him for a while, leads me to believe it could have been just a mishap. Remember when he played golf with the guys at Hilliary Hall that first day out? He let loose of his club and almost hit a player coming up behind us. I'm afraid I was a little angry about his carelessness then. So, I guess I can buy *misadventure*. Unless you know something I don't."

He waited until Claire shook her head.

"Betty's leaving was unusual but there was nothing sinister about it. Her story is really sad, like some you read in the papers and wonder how people are able to cope. Some like Betty aren't able to cope, at least not for a long while.

"That brings us to Tom. Tom with that expensive video camera protruding from his eye was like carrying a sign proclaiming *rich tourist*. It was obviously too tempting for that group of lads." He reached across the table to squeeze her hand. "Something like this happens on a few of our tours each year. I'm just glad it wasn't worse, that they weren't bold enough to go for all your money, and they didn't rough up any of you."

"Tom probably feels like he's been roughed up."

"Of course. But it's probably because he didn't let go fast enough, not that these toughs wanted to do him harm. Because if they had, they would have done a much more thorough job of it."

Claire shuddered.

"Good morning, you two."

Glenda's knowing look, as she waved across the room, caused Claire to realize Jack was still holding on to her hand. She snatched it back, feeling heat rise to her cheeks.

"Well, I've got to finish packing." She rose. "I know, I'll stay out of the stairwells." Then, "Thanks, Jack. Maybe you're right. Maybe I'm making too much of this." And heading toward her room she smiled at and spoke to most of the group's members, who had somehow arrived without her notice.

CHAPTER TWELVE

Painted with glistening green lacquer and trimmed in white and black, its polished brass sent gleams of gold toward the enthralled onlookers. The behemoth steam engine, a relic of the industrial age, dominated the four-story room. The lecturer was discussing its power, its use, the technical terms for each of its parts while the steam engine itself gurgled and pulsed, its power building slowly, like a monster waking from a long sleep. This was the only steam engine left, they were told; one of the largest in all of England. Yet it was only one of several this factory used during the 19th century.

That was when Sheffield was the center of the steel industry. Even now, cutlery, knives and swords branded with the name *Sheffield* meant quality. Whole villages used to be subject to the whims of these monstrous engines, which ran twenty-four hours a day, every day of the week and dictated the events of the lives of those who lived in its shadow.

Currently the factory had been turned into a living museum with a re-creation of a village within its walls, instead of clinging to the outside as it really would have been. The museum provided an accurate glimpse of what the world was like when the steam engine made the industrial revolution possible and workers were expected to keep up with the machine-driven equipment.

Now the noise was building, and the narrator stopped talking, knowing better than to try to compete. The gleaming pistons were turning ever faster with a rhythm of their own. The noise was louder. The throb now matched Claire's heartbeat. It was the sound of her blood coursing through her veins.

Then the pistons became a blur, the noise was all encompassing, people were crowding into the room, jostling each other, drawn to the heartbeat of the village, eyes and mouths wide in wonderment, hypnotized by the sound.

Claire didn't move from her spot until the engine slept again. The sound still echoed in her head as she moved into the darker interior. She wandered down the dirty cobblestone street lined with sparse huts, which made up the squalid little village. The houses were filled with life-sized mannequins posed in the functions of daily living. It was a grim reminder, even with the bits of joy and humor woven into the displays, of how hard life had been not so long ago. At the far end of the village the displays were interspersed with real people, forging steel tools and knives, women baking bread, weaving and running little shops where the goods made on the premises could be sold.

Claire watched the blacksmith working on a pair of iron candelabras, and then moved with the crowd towards the displays of goods manufactured in Sheffield during its industrial reign. Each time the steam engine started up again, the throb vibrated through the floor calling to her, pulling her back. But she resisted, resenting how mesmerized she was by it. Determined to resist its pull she headed out of the museum and found a place at a little refreshment stand near the front door where she had a cool drink and some crisps.

"Are you all through, Claire?" Mrs. Maus sat down at her table beckoning to Joe who was carefully carrying a tray with their lunch on it.

"Yes, if I get anymore attached to that steam engine you'll never get me out of here. I've never seen anything like it."

"Can you imagine how loud it would be with four or five of them going at once? The man said that they don't even turn it on to full power for these demonstrations. No wonder my grandfather was deaf."

Claire looked at Mrs. Maus with interest. "Did your grandfather have something to do with one of these steam engines?"

"Maybe this one." She nodded toward the building. "My father migrated from Sheffield to the States before the Great War—that was World War I. Anyway, when I was about eight, he brought his mother and father over to live with us. I thought they were so old, but in fact they were probably barely in their sixties. That seems pretty young now."

Joe managed to unload the tray on the little table without spilling anything. Mrs. Maus thanked him and reached for a sandwich, but Claire wasn't going to let her get distracted.

"So they came from Sheffield?"

"Papa, that was my grandfather, was totally deaf. So it was hard to communicate with him. When he talked he shouted, poor man. It used to make my littlest brother cry. Papa didn't live long, maybe three years, after he came. But my granny lived until she was ninety-two. She talked a lot about Sheffield. She remembered even the tiniest details until the very end of her life. She had no friends or relatives left who could reminisce with her and I suppose my parents had heard it so many times they were bored. So she told me the stories. You know how kids are; they love to hear stories over and over.

"Granny always said Papa died because they took him away from his engine. He loved his engine more than any thing, she said. He just couldn't live without it."

Claire nodded remembering how the throb became a part of her after only minutes. How would it be after years?

"Papa was an engineer. He was the one that kept the engines going. It was considered an elite job I suppose. They had a better house, and a little more money. But all the houses belonged to the factory. And when you couldn't work anymore, you couldn't live there anymore. Very similar to the company towns in the United States."

Joe nodded. "Some of the mining towns in Utah and Nevada are still like that. Company towns are only for people who work in the mines. The mines subsidize all the stores and services. Remember that old Tennessee Ernie Ford song?" He started humming *Sixteen Tons*.

Claire was shocked. Suddenly it all seemed real. It wasn't all that long ago if Mrs. Maus could remember her granny talking about it. Mrs. Maus' grandfather worked here. If not in this factory, in another one similar to it.

"Anyway he had to be retired and it broke his heart. They didn't have social security then. If you couldn't work, it was your family's responsibility to take care of you. So they came to the States. We lived in New Jersey then. There were a lot of people from Yorkshire in that area, but it wasn't the same for them." She paused a minute, thinking about it.

"I've often thought about what that meant to my mother, taking on her mother-in-law and father-in-law. But that's what people did then. There was no retirement plans. People barely managed to eke out a living, say nothing of saving for their old age or retiring to Florida."

"My mother lived with my family for years, just like my mother's mother lived with us when I was a boy," Joe commented. He finished his sandwich and eyed the other half of Mrs. Maus'. "In fact, when I was a kid in North Beach, every family had some older relative living with them. Each one had some responsibility, like the cooking, or maybe the laundry, or making the wine, or keeping the garden. And they helped look after the kids. Somehow it worked. But, not now. That's not the way it's done anymore." He sounded wistful and then looking up he saw the sympathy in the eyes of Mrs. Maus and Claire. He became a little defensive.

"Well, of course I could live with my son and his wife. They've asked me, over and over. But the truth of the matter is that they live too grandly for my simple needs, and the noise... They have kids all over the place playing loud music. Phones are ringing everywhere.

"Why does any family need a phone in every room?

"And pizza coming to the door." He was getting agitated, waving his hands as he spoke louder with disgust. "I'm just not ready to cope with that kind of life."

Mrs. Maus just looked at him.

"I'm too damn old!"

Her eyes didn't waver, and he squirmed under her look.

"I'm too damn cranky," he finally admitted.

"Cranky?" She laughed accepting his confession. "You know, Joe, cranky can go away. Give up the lonely and, who knows, the cranky just might disappear."

"And, what would I do? They have people to clean the house, people to do the yard, someone to clean the pool. They don't need a grandfather to make wine, or grow zucchini. No, no, I'm better off where I am. My friends understand and we play chess and bocce ball. And we remember."

"Well, I would think that you'd rather spend your last years living, not just remembering. Remembering is fine when you're in the home, strapped into a wheelchair and unable to do anything but drool. You're too young for that, Joe! You should be traveling and sharing your knowledge with your grandchildren and making your wine and growing the zucchini. How do you know your son and his wife wouldn't appreciate it, given the chance?

"And I just told you how important to me it was that my grandmother shared so much of her life with me. You said your grandmother lived with you. Do you have fond memories of her?"

She waited for his nod before continuing. "See, you're depriving your grandchildren of those memories. If things have changed, Joe, you're partly responsible. My grandparents didn't say, 'no, we can't move to America. We have to stay in Sheffield with our friends.' They didn't have any choice, so they went.

"But, you don't want to move a few miles down the Peninsula, because you don't want to change your habits. What about your family?"

Joe grinned sheepishly looking at Claire. "Isn't she something? Doesn't give an inch. The only person I know who's honest enough to say what she thinks."

"Tom, how are you doing?" Mrs. Maus called as he walked past, then turned back to Claire and Joe. "Such a shame. He so enjoyed that camera, and truthfully, I was looking forward to seeing his film when we got back. Now, it's all gone.

"And I can tell his wrist is painful," she added sympathetically.

Joe shook his head. "Kids, today. And you want me to live with a bunch of them?"

"Oh, Joe. Don't be such a curmudgeon. Surely you don't think your grandsons and their friends are anything like the thugs who stole Tom's camera?" Her voice was sharp. She was obviously annoyed with Joe and he knew it.

"No. Of course, not. You're right, Maureen. How could I even say such a thing?" He gave her an apologetic look, and then stood and started stacking the tray with their trash.

* * *

Claire wasn't dozing but she was close. They were headed for Black Swan Inn, the last stop of the trip. She couldn't believe the day after next they would be on the plane again, but this time going home. Already she was starting to prepare herself for real life again. She hated that. She wanted to enjoy every minute up to the time they boarded the plane.

"Well, ladies and gents, this will be your penultimate evening." Jack's voice broke into the naps and musings.

People sat up, looking around expecting that they would be arriving at their hotel at any moment.

Jack smiled diabolically, “Harold and I are going to clean out the storage bins when we unload at the hotel, and everything you’ve purchased and stowed along the way will be delivered to your room.” He grinned at the assorted groans. “That’s right. Somehow between now and Thursday morning you’ll have to make it all a part of your luggage. So I hope you’ve brought some extra totes.”

“Oh, my god. I hope I can squeeze it all in.” Alice really looked worried.

“Well, I helped Betty pack up her things and I’ve got a new appreciation of how much can go into one of these bags. Don’t worry. I’ll come and sit on it for you,” Claire offered.

“Don’t even think about it today.” Florence leaned across the aisle. “It’ll only ruin the evening for you. Plenty of time to worry tomorrow.”

Claire laughed. “Right, Scarlet. Good plan. You know, when we get to the hotel I’m going to have a right proper English Tea one last time. Anyone want to join me?”

Jack commanded their attention once more as he reviewed the schedule for the evening and the next day, finishing just as they pulled into the car park at the picturesque Black Swan Inn.

* * *

“Chatsworth will make all the other great houses you’ve seen look like shacks. And Chatsworth is only one of the houses owned by Bess of Hardwick. Anyone heard of her?” Jack was in his history teacher persona. “Well, ladies and gents, remember in her lifetime women didn't inherit and, except for Queen Elizabeth, they had no power. Bess' father died broke, yet Bess somehow amassed a fortune. She had four husbands, she gave birth to eight children, and raised several more children inherited along with possession from her various husbands. She was imprisoned in the Tower on two different occasions, was a friend and companion to both Queen Elizabeth and Mary, Queen of Scots. She built this grand house, called Chatsworth, and another called Hardwick and owned a few more in the area. When you get home and have more time, Bess' story might be interesting for you to pursue. Was she an early Leona Helmsly?" He paused for added drama. "Or was she a self-made Oprah Winfrey?"

"Oh, look!"

Either by chance or by design, Jack finished just as Chatsworth came in view of the bus. The house nestled in a green blanket of lawns, framed by the river and the surrounding hills. Cameras were whipped out and a flurry of snapping shutters almost drowned out Jack's caution that the mist hadn't yet dissipated and would inhibit them from taking prizewinning photos.

The coach traversed the long drive, heeding the "Look out for Lambs" signs dotting the grass, each minute disclosing yet another view of the house, the grounds, the shooting fountains from the gardens and the peaceful river. Eventually the coach pulled into the car park and found its place between the other coaches, which were also timing their arrival to the opening of the house. The enthusiastic passengers disgorged, chattering excitedly, trying to decide what to see first.

Claire noticed Tom's woebegone face. He was still grieving over the loss of his camera; he seemed lost without it. He had viewed the whole trip through the camera's lens and it was almost like he couldn't see without it. The camera had not been recovered and there had been no opportunity to replace it. At any rate, the record of their trip was gone for good.

She hurried after Rosa, calling out for her to wait. "Rosa, how's it going?"

"Fine, fine. I talked to Lucy last night and she had a couple more things for me but nothing that will keep me from wrapping it all up by the time we leave."

"How was she? Is her leg better?"

Rosa's blank look told Claire that she hadn't even asked.

"Don't worry. I'm sure she's better. I'll be talking to her one last time tonight, so I'll ask her myself." She started to turn towards the house, then paused, turning back to Rosa. "Tonight everyone has decided to meet at the Hound and the Fox in the village for a final dinner. I hope you'll be able to join us."

Rosa was obviously reluctant. "Maybe," she finally muttered. "I really want to get this finished before we leave, so I don't have to work on the plane. Those seats are so narrow there's not much room. And you never know who will be sitting next to you."

Claire nodded. "Well, everyone would appreciate it if you could make it." She didn't know how to break through Rosa's reserve. She had tried to be supportive and friendly, but Rosa seemed determined to stay to herself. Claire knew Lucy had even encouraged her to be part of the group for all the good that did. She had explained it would help identify any issues or omissions in the tour itinerary. But the fact was that when the final draft for Lucy's book was completed Rosa would be leaving and maybe that was what kept her from being friendlier. Well, Lucy would be sorry to lose Rosa, but Claire wouldn't.

* * *

"Sir?" Fenster didn't salute actually, but his greeting was always so formal it seemed he had.

"Well, what the hell is happening? It's been days. What's the story on this group? This Springer Untour?" Ames was grouchy, eager for results. That was the trouble with hope; it raised expectations.

Fenster shook his head. "Nothing. We've seen nothing. We've gone through everything in that bus. And we found nothing." He was disgusted. They spent so much time and effort on this group with no results. What's more it looked like there weren't going to be any results. The group was flying out tomorrow totally ignorant of the scrutiny they had been under, of the reams of reports that contained no clues and the dashed hopes of those they would soon leave behind.

In addition they had delved into the background of every member of the tour, and so far only Charlie Ramsey, alias Arnie White, had any secrets. No one else had even a remote connection that they could pursue.

"Where are they now?"

"Actually, they're probably still at Chatsworth." He glanced at his watch. "Then on for a bit of a tour of the Peak District, then back to the Black Swan in Derby for the night. Tomorrow they make the haul to Heathrow. Not much hope of anything happening now."

"What's the report from your man?"

"He's still uncomfortable with all the oddities but can't make any sense of them. Nor can we."

Fenster grimaced, and tried a touch of levity. "I'm just glad I didn't pay to take that tour, although he says the group is so delighted with the trip they aren't upset about all the problems they've had. And after all, they've not traveled much. Maybe they think this is normal."

Ames sighed, he was not happy. "Well, keep with them to the end. We made a bad decision. Maybe it was a diversion to keep us from watching elsewhere?" He looked at Fenster sharply.

Fenster shifted a little uncomfortably, wishing he had further ideas. But in the end he just shook his head.

"All right, it was a waste. Maybe I'll play golf tomorrow as I planned. But if any thing odd happens, call me."

"Yes, sir." And he escaped. No matter that it was all a big nothing. He still had a million details. They wouldn't relax until the group was gone, and that included the contingent that planned to stay the weekend in London before returning to the States.

They pulled up to the terminal at Heathrow about fifteen minutes ahead of schedule.

"Wait just a moment there, Harold. Don't open the doors just yet." Alex Martinez moved down the aisle to the front of the bus.

"Yoo, Alex."

"Way to go."

"Atta boy, Alex," the others encouraged him to Jack and Harold's surprise.

"Harold here is the best damn coach driver in all of the kingdom." He had to pause for the clapping. "And to show you our appreciation for your skill, Harold, we have commissioned this unique piece of crystal especially for you." He held up the giant beer mug sporting the logo of last night's pub, stuffed with the bank notes everyone had contributed. "And we included a few quid so you could keep it filled."

Harold turned red, not much given to speech. He nonetheless managed a few words of thanks before settling back in his seat.

Annie and Kim squeezed down the aisle past Alex.

"Now Jack, we thought and thought what we could get you to remind you of your best tour group ever."

From the raucous clapping and yelling you would have thought they were back at the pub where they had lingered to the last minute the night before, ignoring the early morning departure looming only hours ahead.

"Anyway, we think we've found the perfect memento."

With a little dramatic pause, Kim whipped out the faded Forty-Niners sweatshirt, laundered to an enviable limpness. Warren had worn it on countless morning runs during the trip, and Jack had admired it openly more than once.

"Don't worry. It's clean," Annie assured him. "And Warren has agreed that for you he will survive without it until he can break in a new one.

"The sweatshirt is from our hearts, but Vern said we had to do something a little more tangible." Kim handed him the fat envelope. "Thank you from all of us for what you added to this trip. We know it wasn't always easy."

The coach almost rocked from the cheers. The bobby directing traffic started over to check them out. Then seeing the laughing faces through the window, shrugged and went back to sorting out the cars, buses and pedestrians.

"You already know that I'm never at a loss for words, but I am overwhelmed with the thoughtfulness of your gift. It's perfect. Just what I've been wanting, at least since the first time I saw it. I appreciate the effort it took for you both to force Warren to give it up."

Annie and Kim hammed it up, bowing to the group. Warren blushed slightly. "It was my pleasure." His grin said it all.

"I'm sure it was." Jack's sardonic reply set everyone off in more peals of laughter.

"I don't know what to say, except if we don't get going you'll all be missing your plane. But seriously, I hope I whet your appetite for England so you'll all want to come back. And when you do, remember to look me up."

When the noise died down he continued, "All right, everyone gather up all your odds and ends, and locate your tickets. Don't leave anything on the coach or Harold will be selling it in Sunday's market in Camden.

"While you're getting yourselves together Harold and I are going to round up luggage carts and get the airline rep, who will get you to the boarding gates."

The next half hour was pretty chaotic. Several of the men helped unload the luggage bins and load the carts Harold had miraculously found. Finally everything was sorted out. Jack introduced them all to Carol Daley, the Vantage Airlines representative.

She gave them a brief explanation of the boarding process and then assured them she would make sure they all got to the proper boarding gate. Several of the women brightened perceptibly when told about the duty-free shops on the other side of the security gates.

"Now if everyone is ready, let's go this way."

She seemed to be a very take-charge person and Claire was more than glad to let her. The Sorinis and the Pedersons were going only as far the taxi stand on the other side as they were going to spend four more days in London before returning to the States. They pushed their carts away from the group in a flurry of waves and last minute comments.

"Well, we never had our dinner."

Claire turned to Jack. “No, we didn’t. Look, Jack, this sounds so inadequate, but thank you. I don’t know how I would have managed without your help.”

“I suspect you would have done just fine.” Jack took her hand. “Nothing else sinister happened?”

“No, you were right.” She smiled brightly, hoping he wouldn’t notice the dark circles under her eyes. She had nightmares again last night. She had been in that warehouse, the bomb was ticking away and she couldn’t get out. She woke up screaming, but finally she realized the pounding she heard wasn’t someone at the door. It was only her heart beating loudly. So maybe she didn’t scream out loud. But she had goose bumps for hours, and she had been happy to stay up those last few hours. She hadn’t wanted any more of that dream.

“Good-bye Claire.” He hugged her briefly, giving her a warm peck on the cheek as he had each of the other women with the exception of Rosa, who had softened only enough to allow him a handshake.

“Oh, hell.” He pulled her back for a real kiss, one she felt all the way to her toes. Releasing her reluctantly he muttered, “I’m really sorry we never had our dinner,” and he winked.

She laughed. Her heartbeat had been cranked up a notch or two and she didn’t try to curb the smile plastered to her face as she pushed her cart into the terminal.

* * *

Claire answered all the questions carefully. The airlines took the check-in process seriously asking if any electronic devices were in her bag, what they were, where the bag had been, when she packed it, how often it had been out of her sight since she packed it, and endless more details. By the time she had secured her boarding pass, the rest of the group had proceeded on to the gates. She hurried to catch up. When she got through the security gates where they X-rayed all the carry on luggage, she was surprised to see Rosa over to the side with two of the security guards in a tense discussion. At least Rosa was tense and her pale complexion looked almost pasty.

"Rosa, what's the matter?"

"Claire, they won't let me take it on unless I run it through the X-ray machine. They say it won't hurt it, but a friend of mine once had her drive deleted and it was a terrible mess. I just can't take the risk."

Claire looked inquiringly at the security guards.

They didn't take her concern seriously. "It's very safe actually. Years ago there may have been a few problems but nowadays people just run them through or boot it up for us here." He gestured to the desk where Rosa's computer case lay with the computer lid open.

"Rosa, can't you just start it up for them. They only want to make sure it's a real computer."

Rosa was very upset. "I can't. It won't start up. I think the battery is dead. It won't boot up."

"Well, can't you just plug it in? I know you brought an adapter plug."

"I packed it." She bit off the words.

Claire could see that she was quite upset.

"I knew I couldn't use it on the plane so why keep it in the case. It just gets in the way if I want to work on the plane."

"Rosa, these men have to do their job. You'll just have to send it through the X-ray."

"I can't. I just can't take a chance. Lucy could lose it all."

Claire was getting impatient with her. "Rosa, you have backup disks, don't you?"

Rosa nodded.

"Then Lucy couldn't lose everything. You'll have to go through the X-rays. That is the rule."

"There you two are. Having a problem, are we?" Carol Daley's accent was as crisp as her smart Vantage uniform.

"I'll need my luggage." Rosa was adamant, explaining to Carol, "Claire doesn't understand. It's not just the data, it's all the systems on the computer that could be screwed up. I'm not taking that chance. I'll have to get the adapter out of my luggage and plug it in."

Carol looked alarmed at that statement. "Your luggage? Oh dear, that will be a problem."

"And if I miss this plane, I'll just have to catch the next. After all that work, I'm not doing anything to risk losing it."

Claire tried to explain to Carol. "She means it. She has been working on the computer for the entire trip, entering data. She's very thorough. She won't take a chance on losing it. Is there any possibility of getting her suitcase back?"

"Of course, we can. But it will take some time and it could result in delaying your flight."

"I don't know what else we can do."

Carol looked at Rosa, then the computer. "The X-ray is really quite safe. Won't you trust us? It would be so simple."

Rosa's expression was set stubbornly; she wasn't giving an inch.

Claire grimaced. "She's been so protective of that laptop through the whole trip and wouldn't let anyone touch it. It's her responsibility, you see. She's using it to record the data she's checked for Lucy Springer's book. Have you heard of Lucy? She's fairly well known in the travel book crowd."

Carol nodded. "Actually, that's why I'm here. She's given our company some nice publicity over the years and the word came down from public relations in the States to make sure everything goes smoothly for your group."

She seemed to make up her mind, and stepped to the side to confer with the security men. One of them finally turned away and called someone on his little handset. Soon another man arrived and had a conversation with Carol and the two security attendants. He then examined the opened computer, even lifting the top to peer at the battery pack and the wiring boards. Then miraculously, he nodded.

Rosa was profusely grateful when the security guards motioned to her to pack up her case. She moved towards the passport control station that Carol pointed her to, but not without Claire seeing a flash of triumph on her face as she turned away from them. That really annoyed her, and she wondered if Rosa just made things difficult for the pleasure of winning the ensuing battle. But then watching her protectively carrying the laptop, she shrugged, deciding Rosa was just strange.

* * *

"Everyone accounted for?" Claire plopped down in a seat across from Joe, Mrs. Maus and Rosa, easing the backpack off her shoulder and setting the stuffed Vantage Airline tote at her feet.

She looked around. Seeing George and Florence Mohney sitting with Kim, Annie and Warren over a couple of rows, she waved to them. Vern and Mike were talking to Alex and Glenda near the entrance to the jetway.

"I don't see Alice or Teri and Shar," she said with a little worry.

"Our shoppers? Don't worry, there's plenty of time. They've only started with the first class check-in." Mrs. Maus, chipper as usual, didn't seem to be bothered by their early morning departure like Joe. His eyes were already at half-mast.

"Where are you sitting, dear?"

Claire checked her ticket. "I'm 18B. On the aisle and not too far back."

"13C," Rosa responded when Mrs. Maus looked her way.

"Oh, you're both near the front. Joe is too. He's 17C, but I'm 35A. A window. I love to see the world and we're going over the top you know. I'm hoping there won't be too many clouds. I'd like to see Greenland.

"And of course I'm close to the loo." She laughed. "Such a fun name for it.

"It's been such a wonderful trip and it's been wonderful of you both to take such good care of us in Lucy's absence." She smiled warmly at Rosa and Claire.

Rosa glanced at her watch and then stood up. "You know, speaking of Lucy, I think I have just enough time to dash over to that shop and pick up some ginger biscuits for her. She loves them." She looked at the computer case lying by her feet, then at Joe. "Joe, would you keep an eye on this for me? I won't be long."

"Of course, don't worry. If we board before you get back, I'll just put it down by my feet until you retrieve it."

Rosa looked uncertain.

"Go along, Rosa. Joe will take good care of it. It's too heavy to be carrying around when you want to do some fast shopping," Mrs. Maus encouraged her.

Rosa nodded hesitantly. "Well, I won't be long, but I will be getting on last. I want to be certain everyone is boarded."

Rosa had barely been swallowed up in the crowd hurrying from one duty-free shop to another, when they heard the announcement for preboarding.

"Mrs. Maus, why don't you preboard? You're way in the back and you could get settled before the crowd."

"I don't need any special help, dear."

"Of course not, but who would know? You have gray hair and you carry a cane. I'm sure no one would ever suspect what a dynamo you really are."

Even Joe woke up enough to laugh at that.

"Let's." He started gathering up his tote and coat, slinging the strap of the laptop over his shoulder. "We should take advantage of the few benefits allotted the aging. And I'll get a real snooze while everyone else gets on board." He crooked his elbow gallantly. "I'll be your escort, my dear." They headed for the door of the Jetway.

"There you are, Claire. Oh, they have the nicest stores here. Why there is even a branch of Harrod's down the way a piece." Shar was laden with parcels she dumped on the seats Joe and Mrs. Maus had just vacated. She and Teri began combining bags and repacking their tote bags. They had all been warned that they would not be allowed on with more than two bags.

"But surely, that doesn't include our purses?"

Alice nodded. "Carol said it did. You bought too much. You'll just have to leave it here."

They all burst into laughter at Shar's horrified expression.

"Look, Shar. Put your purse in that big shopping bag. Then you'll only have two," Claire suggested. So, by the time their seat numbers were called, they each had only two bulky bags.

Claire stored her tote above. She had a sweater and her book in her backpack, which she was using as a purse. The young girl in the window seat was already curled up with a pillow and blanket. She smiled in greeting as Claire got her seatbelt untangled and fastened, but then snuggled down again for a serious sleep. Eventually, the plane was loaded, and they pushed back from the gate. The cabin lights had dimmed and everyone but the most experienced travelers had sat back, quietly tense, just waiting until the plane successfully became airborne.

Claire could see Joe a seat ahead of her and across the aisle. He was sleeping soundly—so soundly that when the other passengers came to his row, they invariably went around and came in the other aisle rather than wake him. She wished she could do that. She was really tired now. The late night, then the nightmare and the sleepless hours after, coupled with the long drive and the exhaustion of getting on the plane wiped her out. She was having a hard time keeping her eyes open. But she fought sleep, she was still afraid of the dreams.

She didn't understand why she was having so many nightmares during this trip? They had almost gone away during the past year. Now they were back worse than ever.

And that bomb ticking last night. There had never been a bomb, at least a ticking one. And she hadn't known when she was in the warehouse that it was just minutes away from bursting into flames. But that ticking bomb in her dream had been so real that when she woke, and she had calmed down a little, she had searched her room for a source of the ticking. But of course it had all been in her head.

Joe snorted.

Claire smiled, wondering if he was going to snore the whole trip. He had certainly changed for the better on this trip. When they started, everyone thought he was a real grouch. He had turned out to be a pussycat. But maybe he had always been, if you got to know him.

She noticed that he still had the laptop bag tucked protectively under the seat in front of him. She looked up the aisle for Rosa, but she didn't see her. She sat up, looking more carefully, sure that Rosa said she was sitting only a few seats in front of Joe.

But there was no one in an aisle seat that even remotely resembled Rosa. Rosa's unique looks would be hard to mistake. And while the plane was not entirely filled, all the window and aisle seats were taken.

Where could Rosa be? Surely she wouldn't have changed seats. Besides if there had been problem with her seat, knowing Rosa, Claire wouldn't have missed the resulting commotion.

The plane was still taxiing and the flight attendants were nowhere to be seen, probably already strapped in their little jump seats. Claire sat back, trying to be logical. Rosa had to be onboard. She must have been mistaken about her seat number.

But, Rosa had her boarding pass in her hand when she told Mrs. Maus where she was sitting. Claire was sure it was 13C. Claire looked down the aisle again counting from Joe's seat. No, 13C held a plump, redheaded woman, and the seat in front and in back were both occupied by men.

If Rosa was sitting behind them, Claire would have seen her pass. And there was no way she would have passed Joe without claiming her computer. After two weeks of traveling with the woman, Claire was sure of that. She could be in front on the other side. Maybe, her ticket was E or even G that sounded a lot like C. Maybe, Claire misunderstood. That was probably what happened.

Claire relaxed a bit. She was just being silly. Then her eyes fell on Joe again, traveling down to his feet and the precious laptop that Rosa wouldn't even let them X-ray for fear of causing it damage. Wasn't that just like Rosa to make such a big fuss over simple procedures? They X-rayed everything. They were serious about their security precautions. But they didn't X-ray the laptop. Which was now sitting at Joe's feet and Rosa was nowhere to be seen.

Claire's heart lurched so hard that the laptop she was staring at started to disappear into blackness. Her scalp tingled as if her hair was electrified. She gripped the armrests, digging her fingers in to keep upright and blinked rapidly, trying to clear her vision. She couldn't breathe!

She was gasping as she fumbled with her seatbelt. She had to get free. She had to stop them.

* * *

Fenster stood at the window until the plane pushed back from the jetway and started rolling toward the runway.

"Well, nothing!" He slammed his fist against the sill. "Nothing, damn it.

"What went wrong? Did that fiasco with Ramsey scare them off, or wasn't there ever anything to it?"

The man beside him shrugged as they turned from the window. That's the way things went in this business. Weeks of endless checking, endless preparation and then sometimes nothing came of it. It was the way things worked.

"Well, Jack, at least you got a little vacation out of it." Fenster put his hand on Jack's shoulder. "Huh, good job for you when you retire, hey?"

"Sure, some vacation. Running around day and night, checking on everyone, memorizing facts and history for the next day and being pleasant at all costs." He made a face.

"Ah, the hardest part. Being pleasant. I understand that there were several attractive single ladies included. It must have been difficult." He laughed, already recovered from his disappointment. After all, it was part of the job. Now he was wondering how he was going to justify all the expenses for Ames. He should have never suggested it had anything to do with Guiness. Guiness was a major button in Ames' makeup. He had spent years failing to capture Guiness, or even coming close to identifying him.

Guiness was wily. Guiness was deadly. Guiness was successful.

Fenster wondered one more time if there really was a Guiness, or if the terrorists just used that name for a successful coup, leaving the authorities chasing a shadow.

He felt the tickle of vibration from the phone tucked in his belt. "Fenster, here."

"What?" He stopped dead, reaching out his hand to halt Jack.

"Jack, there is some disturbance on Vantage Flight 1092." He turned back to the phone while Jack tried to contain his impatience.

"Something about Rosa not being onboard, but her computer is."

Jack's face darkened. "Rosa would never be separated from that computer. Are you sure Rosa isn't onboard?"

Fenster talked into the phone. They both ignored the people swerving around them in the crowded terminal.

"There is no Rosa Marino on the manifest!"

They looked at one another for a moment. Then Fenster barked into the phone, "Tell them to get that plane evacuated. And run another check on Rosa Morino. She was in the boarding area. She had a ticket.

"We need to get out there." He paused looking around to locate the gate he was being directed to by the voice on the phone. Pointing for Jack's benefit, they both started moving rapidly down the corridor. When they moved further from the duty-free shops the congestion thinned out enough to run, the phone still stuck to Fenster's ear. Jack was right behind him.

They had their ID's out for the guard at the door and when they burst out into the daylight, a car came to a sliding stop at the bottom of the stairs just long enough for them to tumble in.

Jack sat back, glad for the expertise of the driver skidding around planes and maintenance trucks, shooting across runways, seeming to know exactly where he was going.

"Get Rosa's picture circulated and don't let anyone leave the boarding area. I don't care how much of a problem that is. Remind them it might be Guiness' work." Fenster shouted into the phone.

Jack listened to Fenster barking orders, as if he was in charge on United States soil, instead of just a guest tolerated as a courtesy. He knew for all Fenster's orders to his staff, the British were very well prepared to handle this kind of emergency, probably better than any American was. They had control and they would brook no interference.

Jack was actually cursing at himself. How could Rosa have fooled him? Sure, she had been checked out. But, somehow, something had been missed. And he had been there. He should have noticed something.

Unless...

Unless, something had happened to Rosa. Could she have been kidnapped?

No, he shook his head. She would have been on the manifest. She would have been listed as a no-show. And her luggage would have been checked-in. It would have caused a big problem to have a no-show with luggage onboard. They would have halted the flight for that.

And Fenster said she wasn't on the manifest, and she wasn't on the plane. That meant it was arranged. It was planned, and it had to have taken place right under his nose.

CHAPTER FOURTEEN

Claire clung just inside the little galley, barely managing to stay upright when the huge plane turned sharply right, eliciting gasps of surprise from the cabin. Then an unnatural stillness settled as the flight attendant started talking over the microphone. People paid attention, removing their glasses and shoes, nudging sleeping neighbors, looking around as instructed to locate the nearest exit. No one spoke. Everyone seemed calm, somehow resigned to their fate.

The flight attendant's voice became even louder, more authoritative as the plane came to a halt and other attendants down the length of the plane struggled with the doors and the exit slides. The seatbelts were all unbuckled at the same time, with the resounding click vibrating through the silence in the cabin. People stood up and moved quickly, but in an orderly manner, towards the exits. It was unreal, not at all like it was on disembarking when people fought each other to get the luggage bins opened, jockeying for a better position in the aisle to get out faster, creating clogs that slowed down the process.

No luggage now, no coats or jackets, no shoes or glasses. All small children were being carried.

Noise was drifting in through the open doors competing with the silence inside, interfering with the concentration as each person came to the slide straining to hear the flight attendants' instructions. Jump, feet first, try to remain upright in a sitting position. When your feet hit the ground, don't hesitate. Run as fast and as far as possible.

Claire was dancing with impatience. Hurry, hurry, she wanted to urge them. Faster! But the flight attendants were in control. They were following procedures.

There went Joe!

She saw Annie and Kim at the door on the other side. The others must be leaving through different exits. She worried momentarily about Mrs. Maus. Would they let her take her cane? How could she run without it?

The flight attendant now motioned to her to get in line. She was surprised that the plane was almost empty.

She had been told she had to wait. They weren't through with her yet. They didn't want to believe her. But she was frantic and somehow she had convinced them. The plane abruptly turned in another direction giving up its place in line. She couldn't blame them for their skepticism. She probably seemed demented. She wasn't sure she was even coherent, insisting they stop and get everyone off. All the while, the flight attendants kept trying to get her to sit down for takeoff.

Now at the door she could see emergency vehicles parked around the perimeter of the area. Dozens of people were helping passengers off the slides, propelling them as quickly as possible to minibuses. More vehicles were arriving and more buses. It looked very confusing, but then

Claire was on the slide, trying to remain upright, feet first just like the instructions. One of the male flight attendants went past her sideways. A larger person obviously goes faster, and somehow he had gotten out of control. She didn't see him land. She was too busy herself when she reached the bottom in a heap, and hands grabbed her on both sides. She was running over the rough, cold cement. She had no choice but to keep up with her guides. She didn't care. She wanted to run. She wanted to get away.

But instead of heading for the nearest minibus they led her towards a car.

"Ms. Gulliver?" one man inquired politely. At her nod he opened the back door for her. The car took off in a burst of speed as soon as the doors closed.

Claire craned her head to see the plane, but no more people were coming down the slides.

The car she was in followed the buses for a while and then veered off to stop near a staircase in the terminal.

"This way." The men were brusque, striding rapidly, giving her no time for questions. She was short of breath when they reached their destination.

It was a small lounge of some kind. No windows, a few doors and no heat. Claire shivered. She was cold and scared. She headed for the couch and then remembering, she slipped off the backpack she had fastened to her chest while she was waiting in the galley. It must have been in her hands when she ran to the front to stop the plane, and it seemed senseless to just leave it in the galley. It had her sweater, her passport and now her shoes. She slipped on the shoes and pulled the sweater over her head, feeling a little warmer, but no less frightened.

"We just have to ask a few questions." It went on for hours, but it was probably less than one. They were very polite, not really threatening, but she felt threatened.

When they left, they assured her they would be back. Soon after, a man wheeled in a cart with tea fixings and even a couple of plates of sandwiches. After he left, Claire opened the door. There was a uniformed guard outside.

"Yes miss? Can I help you?"

"The loo? I need the loo." She stammered a little, wondering if she was under arrest.

The young guard was very serious, no hint of a smile. He opened the door wider and pointed to one of the doors in the lounge.

After making use of the facilities, she helped herself to tea and some sandwiches. It wasn't until after the second cup that she started to explore her surroundings. No TV or radio, a few old magazines, all doors were locked except for the toilet and the one she used to enter. No other way to exit.

But she didn't need another exit, did she? Surely, that guard would provide for her safety. But if she was in danger and she had to hide, there was nowhere in this lounge to hide, nowhere she could protect herself.

She wondered what was happening at the plane.

She wondered if everyone got off without mishaps and if they knew more than she did.

She was nervous. Where was everyone? Why didn't they tell her anything? Were her friends okay?

Maybe there was a simple explanation for this whole thing, and she was going to look like a fool.

Maybe she was crazy.

Suddenly she was certain she had made a mistake, an awful, costly, embarrassing mistake.

What was the penalty for turning in a false alarm? She remembered newspaper stories of evacuations. There were always broken bones and sprains—she shuddered—and sometimes heart attacks.

She poked her head out the door. “I just wondered if you had any news.”

The young man was stern, shaking his head, closing the door in her face.

“Well, thank you for your concern,” Claire muttered. She went back to the sofa and in an effort to keep busy she emptied her backpack on the table, sorting through the bits of receipts, gum wrappers, ticket stubs and paper tissues, limp from being crushed amongst the contents. When she moved the bag she was surprised to feel heaviness on one side. She explored the side pocket and came out with the packet of Arnie's pictures she had shoved in there in Conwy and then completely forgotten.

She picked them up, fighting back tears at the memory. She should have turned them over to the police to be sent back with Arnie's things.

She opened up the first package, clearly taken in the early days of the trip. Then she stared at her face. Her mouth was unattractively opened, her eyes startled, something blurred at her chin.

She looked closer and saw Vern beside her. It was the morning they left London. This was that picture Liz took of her at breakfast.

Why did Arnie have Liz's pictures?

She heard voices at the door and laid the pictures down half rising when Jack came through the door with another man following him.

"Jack, what are you doing here?" She paused, her voice cracked. "Oh, I'm really in trouble, aren't I?"

She hurried across the room, her distress choking her. "I don't know what got into me.

"I was so sure. And I was really scared. I didn't know what to do, but I had to do something. You understand, don't you? Please." She was twisting her hands, trying to make him, them, understand. "Please, I didn't mean any harm. Tell them. Tell them I'm not a crazy.

"It was those nightmares about bombs. I don't know why, really. Rather, I do know why, but I don't know why bombs."

Jack grabbed her hands, forcing them to be still. "Claire..."

"What will they do to me? No one was hurt, were they? Tell me Mrs. Maus is okay."

"Claire, they found the bomb."

His voice seemed to be coming through water. She heard someone say, "Grab her. She's going over."

Next she knew, she was on the couch, and Jack was trying to get her to drink some vile tepid drink that turned out to be the dregs from the teapot.

She shook her head and straightened up.

"I'm fine. Really, I'm fine." She struggled to control her voice, determined to convince them she was fine, while still fighting the darkness pressing down at the back of her eyes.

"I was just shocked, you know. I had just decided that I was wrong, and then when I saw you, I thought I was really in trouble." She rattled on. Then looking at Jack, "Why are you here Jack? We said good-bye hours ago. Didn't you have to get back to the office or something to make a report?"

Jack looked a little embarrassed, but the man with him wasn't. "Jack doesn't really work for Kingdom Tours. He was there to keep an eye on things for us."

Before Claire could actually digest this, the door opened and several people came in the room, proceeding to the locked doors she had tried earlier. One room was a large workroom containing desks, tables, phones and assorted equipment. The second room contained a kitchen including a table and chairs. She watched with amazement as people sat down and started working as if they had always been there. A woman wheeled a laden cart into the kitchen and soon the delicious smell of coffee wafted through the room.

The man with Jack was talking to an authoritative man, but she couldn't follow the conversation. She felt a little dazed, like she was in Wonderland. Things weren't quite making sense.

"Jack, what about the bomb?"

Jack couldn't hide the surprise on his face. He had forgotten her. "You were right. It was the computer she had been hauling around. At least the case was. Inside was a very unique bomb, with plastic explosives in place of the battery pack. It looked just like a computer but it was rigged to go off about three hours after takeoff." He glanced at his watch. "Just about now you would have all been bits and pieces falling in the sea."

Claire shuddered. Sick to her stomach she lurched to the loo with no time to spare. Finally, her stomach empty, the heaves under control, she repeatedly bathed her face until she felt she could control her shaking enough to allow her to return.

A new group of people wanted to go over it one more time, and then back over it again. Every time she got to the part about going through security they almost lost it. One of the men, tersely issued orders to a subordinate, and Claire thought dismally that Carol Daley's career with Vantage Airlines was surely over. Claire hoped that was the worst of what would happen to her. And then there were the security guards and their supervisor, who approved the exception. These were people whose only failing was trying to please everyone. These were people, who had been used by Rosa. Yet, their attempt at kindness almost allowed a planeload of people to disappear without a trace. Who would have ever known what happened?

Claire didn't know how much time had elapsed, but she was nervously trying some saltines with a cup of black tea, hoping to settle her stomach.

"No one recognized the picture of Rosa. They reviewed the tape of everyone going through passport control, but didn't see her," Jack reported grimly.

"But, that's impossible. I went through passport control the same time she did. I sat with her at the boarding gate. They either missed her, or they didn't take her picture."

"They have everyone's picture. It's standard procedure."

"Well, let me see the picture they're using for I.D. Maybe it's old and she's changed since it was taken."

"Good idea." Jack directed himself to the man who came in with him. "Fenster, let us look at the picture you're using. Maybe it's not a good likeness."

"Ian, bring that photo of Rosa here," the man with Fenster bellowed into the other room.

A young, painfully thin, redhead rushed over with a sheaf of photos.

Jack and Claire looked up amazed. "This isn't Rosa," they chorused.

"What?"

Jack shook his head. "This is not Rosa Morino. How could you have made such a mistake?"

Everyone looked at Ian, who seemed to shrink within himself. "That's Rosa Morino," he said tentatively, then stronger, "It's Rosa Morino. It came from the U.S. Passport Office."

Claire looked at it again. The fiftyish, graying blonde, slightly overweight woman in the photo was exactly how she had pictured Rosa Morino before she arrived at Lucy's doorstep.

"Well, whoever this is, it isn't the person who has been traveling with us as Rosa Morino." Jack was emphatic.

"And this isn't the person who has been working with Lucy Springer for the past several months. Could there be another Rosa Morino? I suppose it isn't that unique of a name."

Ian consulted the notes under the stack of pictures. "This Rosa Morino is fifty-three years old, has worked as an editor for some very prestigious New York publishing houses before returning ten years ago to her family home in Aubrie, North Carolina. She took a temporary assignment in California several months ago as a special favor for an old friend."

Claire opened her mouth, then closed it, finding that she didn't really have anything to say.

The men cast grim looks at each other, and the one who seemed to be in charge said what they were all thinking. “Doesn’t sound good for this Rosa Morino.

“Fenster, better get your blokes checking for unidentified bodies.” Then looking at Jack and Claire he said, “Perhaps you two would care to review the tape for us. That way we can identify this person we’re looking for.” He paused. Remembering his manners, he pulled a card from this inner suit pocket and handed it to Claire.

“I apologize for my rudeness, Ms. Gulliver. I’m Nigel Smythe-Cook. I can’t tell you how much we appreciate your warning. I hope you are willing to work with us on this.”

Jack seemed to wake up. “Sorry, Claire. This is Bert Fenster. He’s attached to the American Embassy.” He gestured towards the man with him.

“Ian Flemming.” The young man held out his hand. “No relation to the real Ian Flemming you know.”

“Ian, get that tape and monitor set up over there,” Smythe-Cook ordered. The pleasantries were over and now he was all business. “I’m afraid it’s rather a tedious process, Ms. Gulliver, but I guarantee if she went through passport control, she’s on this tape.”

Claire could hardly keep her eyes open. She pulled herself sharply upright, determined to be alert for Rosa. But it was hard when she knew Jack would recognize Rosa, even if she snoozed.

“Jack, wait. Go back. Did you see that guy?”

Jack poked the reverse button.

“There, there. Don’t you recognize him?” Claire had a puzzled look on her face. “That’s really weird. That’s the same guy we saw on the road when we got stuck with the lorry. Remember?”

Jack shook his head. “Never saw him.”

“I’m sure it’s him.” She was talking faster now. “Rosa handled him. He tried to go around out of turn but Rosa cut him off. She talked to him a while and he seemed to calm down and he waited for his turn.”

Her eyes widened as she remembered. “We saw him in the pub that night in Conwy.” Her tone was hushed. “He was there that night. The night Arnie died. Mike went over to buy him a drink to make up for the inconvenience we caused on the road, but he wasn’t friendly. He just got up and left.”

Her face reflected horror as she whispered, “He left, and Arnie died.”

Ian wrote something on his pad and then went in the other room. Nigel came out with Fenster right behind them.

They watched the man Claire recognized several times before setting the VCR on pause, so they all could examine every detail of his face.

“He’s American,” Claire remembered. “Mike said he was an American.”

“A bit too much of a coincidence, wouldn’t you say, Fenster?”

Fenster nodded.

“Good work, Ms. Gulliver. Carry on while we check up on our friend here.”

Jack started the play button again. Ian was back with them. Claire was wide awake now.

“How will they find out who that guy was?” Claire whispered.

Ian answered. “See those numbers running across the bottom of the tape? Those are exact times. We run them against the computer inputs to identify the passport origin and number."

"I didn't notice them keying the numbers in a computer."

Ian looked smug.

"They don't. They have their ways. Very useful on occasion," Jack explained, turning his attention back to the screen.

"Look, there is Vern... and Mike."

For the next fifteen minutes they saw all the members of the tour pass through passport control.

"There she is. That's Rosa."

Claire was shocked at how sinister Rosa looked. Before today she had thought her a humorless, dour and dedicated woman. Now the video revealed a cruel-looking person—a person who was planning to blow up hundreds of innocent people. How could they have not seen it all those days they were together?

Claire couldn't control her shaking. "How could she? Why would she want to harm any of us? What kind of person can eat, travel, and be intimate with people while all the time planning to kill them."

"We intend to find out in just about three hours."

Nigel and Fenster had joined them.

"Rosa and Edward Karlosky, also known as Barry Kilpatrick, are on Vantage Flight 834 landing at Miami. This flight took off four plane spaces in front of yours, so there is no way they know their target was diverted."

Fenster's smile was so menacing Claire couldn't stop the shiver running up her spine. "We'll be waiting for them."

"What the Hell happened?" The anger was apparent and panic made the voice shrill.

"N-N-Nothing," his stutter came from shock, his mind casting around for an answer.

Now heavy sarcasm. "I know that. The flight was canceled. Canceled! That's a euphemism for 'the bomb was discovered'."

He almost dropped the receiver. His heart was racing. He couldn't get his breath. It couldn't be!

The sarcasm continued, "Don't worry, you said! The best in the business, she said! Hell, you people are rank amateurs!"

Now the words were low, barely above a whisper and furious. "I'm ruined. You realize that, don't you? After all my careful planning. And all that money?" The voice ran out of steam, paused, then became calculating. "So where is our friend? I have a few words for her ears."

"She's on her way. Her plane will land shortly," he answered defensively. Then, because he couldn't believe they failed, "Are you sure? I've got the BBC news on and there hasn't been a word."

"Hah. No word about a plane going down either, I'll wager." The sneer grated. "It's no wonder your cause is so hopeless. You can't do anything right."

The receiver was dead in his hand.

Amateurs?

He had dared to call them amateurs.

He sat still a minute thinking it through, testing the idea that their plan had somehow failed. Of course it had been risky. Guiness only agreed to take part, because the plan was so bold it could have worked. Who would suspect the innocuous tour group from California to include one of the world's most wanted terrorists? And Guiness knew that even the strictest procedures and strongest controls would break down easiest under the pressure of human kindness—someone trying to be helpful, or someone doing a favor for someone. That was why they decided the plan had a good chance for success.

But, he admitted with a sinking sensation, a fact he should have noticed before the phone call, there had been no news of the plane going down.

So it had not. And the American would have known if it had. He was in the best position to hear.

So they had failed. Well, they knew that was possible. But now what? Was Guiness on the plane? Did she know the plan failed? Was she expecting him to protect her when she landed?

He had to assume she was on the plane. If she knew it was aborted or if part of the plan failed, she would have used one of their alternate plans and he would have already heard from her. So she didn't know.

All right, he decided, it was up to him to plan some surprises for anyone planning one for Guiness.

"Ned, get the others in here. We have some work to do," he called. And later, after they were all safe, then he would tell Guiness what the stupid American said. He grinned evilly, anticipating her reaction.

* * *

Claire rifled through the pictures on the coffee table. Two packets of pictures had obviously belonged to Liz. There were Liz's candid shots, mostly of people with surprised looks from the flash, as well as several pictures of Rosa. One was of Rosa at the Camden Locks market. Claire remembered that incident. There was a full face picture of a man walking away from her, but it was not apparent if he had been talking to her or not. At the end of the second packet, Liz caught Rosa again in Bath and it was obvious that her friend, Barry Kilpatrick, had met her there. He was clearly recognizable.

So much for Liz's righteous denial of having taken Rosa's picture. She had been lying just as Rosa claimed. Still, Liz had it right from the beginning and Claire uncomfortably remembered her own cavalier dismissal of Liz's accusations. Maybe Rosa pushed Liz down the steps just as she claimed. Claire wondered at her own intuitive powers. How could she have failed to see what was going on under her nose?

The other packet of pictures had been Arnie's. The camera work was almost professional in quality. These were not tourist shots, no scenery or tour members waving in front of historic buildings. No, he had somehow managed to surreptitiously obtain a full face picture of everyone in the group. Claire didn't even remember when he had taken the one of her.

"What have you there?" Ian paused on the way to fill his cup, looking at the pictures spread out on the table.

When Claire explained, he called in to Jack.

Jack and Fenster carefully reviewed them. When they got to the picture Arnie had taken of Rosa, Fenster commented, "Well, Jack, perhaps Ramsey was more competent than we gave him credit for. I'd guess we misjudged him by accepting that verdict of *misadventure* for his accident."

Claire felt the blood draining from her face. She tried to steady herself but blackness engulfed her once more.

Jack grabbed her head and forced it down to her knee level. She fought against the awkward position. But then the lightheaded feeling began to recede and she relaxed. A few moments more and he let go. She sat up and glared at Jack. "So you did know each other, that first morning getting on the bus?"

He shrugged almost sheepishly. "I don't know which of us was more surprised. Arnie White was an alias. His real name was Charlie Ramsey. I had been in the same class in the academy with him. He was smart and totally dedicated, but he couldn't qualify for fieldwork. It was a major disappointment to him. Most cadets opt out when that happens, but he chose to work in a different capacity and still be a part of the group. He was working at a monitoring station in your area when he picked up some information he believed was connected to your tour. His boss didn't take it seriously so he decided to take some vacation time and follow it up himself.

"Charlie had no business in the field and he knew it. Then you caught us in the garden at Castle Combe. That's what you heard us arguing about. He refused to go back. He said he was on his own time, spending his own money."

Jack looked frustrated. "He didn't always use good sense and he was always bungling things. I was afraid he would tip our hand. But he was certain that Guiness was there, and he was going to be in on his capture."

"Guiness? Who's Guiness?"

Fenster explained, "Guiness is the leader of a fringe Irish terrorist group that has been operating successfully for the past twenty odd years. We have never been able to identify more than one or two minor players, so we have no clue as to who Guiness really is. He seems to be as much a secret to the other terrorists as he is to us. We think Rosa and her friend are part of his group. And, thanks to you Claire, this scheme of theirs didn't work out quite the way they planned." Fenster's face softened with gratitude.

Claire was having trouble adjusting to the idea that Arnie was some kind of secret agent. Arnie was definitely not a James Bond, more like a Maxwell Smart, she conceded. And he died because he was getting too close to his target. The whole situation boggled her mind. It was very much like a bad movie.

She shuddered. And Rosa was an international terrorist? Closely placed to one of the world's most sought after criminals?

"Shouldn't we be hearing from Miami?" Jack asked, checking his watch. Then picking up the pictures, he and Fenster headed back into the control room, leaving Claire to get used to all this unpleasant information.

* * *

"Lucy, it's Claire. Look, we've had a little delay." Claire forged ahead, wanting to get it all out and over, not giving Lucy a chance to reply. "Actually, the flight was canceled and I didn't want you to get to the airport and then worry because our plane wasn't scheduled."

She suddenly realized Lucy hadn't said a word. "Lucy, are you okay?"

"Hardly. These people are driving me crazy." The voice was clear and angry.

"What people? What's going on?"

"I've had these people here for hours. They're making a mess of things. They're swarming over the guesthouse. They've taken every single thing Rosa left in there, and they are asking me endless questions—over and over, like I won't remember that they have asked the same thing sixteen different ways." Her voice got stronger. "And do they answer any of mine? Of course not!

"Claire, what on earth is going on about Rosa? Do you know? Is she there? I keep trying to tell them that she's harmless and how highly she was recommended to me. But they don't believe me."

Lucy's voice echoed her rage, continuing, "And now they say the accident on the back porch wasn't an accident at all. Someone tampered with the step. They showed me."

"Oh, no!" Claire protested weakly, already believing it after what she had recently learned.

"They say Rosa sent me out there with that story about that big tom being after Fluffy again, and I fell for it. And subsequently, right down the steps. I could have been killed! And why? They think she wanted to take my place on the trip."

Claire was horrified. "But, what if we had canceled the trip. I wanted to, as you well know."

Lucy replied thoughtfully, "That was part of the risk. She was gambling on us going. We were so close to the departure date and everything was ready for us to leave, so it didn't make sense to cancel. And she was right. We did just what she wanted. We behaved just as she planned.

"Christ, I was so grateful to her for her work, I probably would have taken her with us if she'd asked. So why was all this intrigue necessary?

"Do you know where she is?" Lucy wheedled. "I'd sure like to talk to her, better yet, get my hands on her for about five minutes."

"I haven't seen her since we got to the airport, honest!" Claire's mind was racing, sorting out those things she could share with Lucy and those she couldn't.

"Listen Lucy, it sounds like you have your hands full there. Don't worry about us. Jack tells me that no one was hurt. At least not seriously."

"Hurt? What are you talking about?" Lucy's voice raised several octaves, demanding, "Claire Gulliver, you tell me everything you know, right now."

Now Claire was caught. She needed to get off the phone quickly before she did any more damage. She explained how the plane had to be evacuated due to an emergency situation, specifically omitting any reference to a bomb, as she had been instructed to do by Fenster.

"So you see Lucy, that's why the flight was canceled. They are sending everyone back to the States as space is available on various airlines but we don't know who will go when.

"I was hoping you would call my mother and Mrs. B for me." Her voice trailed off, uncertain. "I didn't realize that you would be in the middle of an investigation." But, Claire thought, she should have realized that.

"Oh, Claire, I'm sorry I'm so whiny. Of course I'll call them. After all, this whole mess is my fault. I feel so guilty about getting you into this. I swear, with all my travels, I have never had any of these things happen to me. I just don't understand what happened.

"I'll call them both right after I hang up with you. What do you want me to say?"

"Lucy, you didn't cause any of this to happen. Please don't blame yourself. You were a victim. But, I would really appreciate your calling my mother. You know how she is. She'll have so many questions, I'd never get off the phone.

"Now don't say anything about Rosa or the plane. Let her think I decided to stay a few more days. And tell Mrs. B I'll call her Sunday or Monday and let her know when I'm coming back."

"Of course. And don't worry about what I'll say about Rosa. I don't know anything about Rosa and obviously no one is going to tell me." The injured tone made Claire feel guilty. "These people have given me instructions. Frankly I'm surprised they let me talk to you. But you won't tell me anything, will you?"

Claire knew she couldn't hold out long, so she promised to call Lucy again as soon as she learned when she would be returning, and hung up.

"Did you know that Lucy's house is swarming with people checking for fingerprints and clues? Did you know her fall down the steps was not an accident? The step had been tampered with." Jack was sitting near her, and Claire was sure it was to make certain she didn't say too much.

"No, I didn't know, but I can't say I'm surprised. After all, once we found out about Rosa it put everything in a different light, didn't it?"

Claire nodded. Then said with surprise, "Of course, I just hadn't gotten that far."

"Look, Claire. We need you to go over your story again. This time we'll video tape you. Think you can get through it?"

Claire shivered. She didn't want to do it again, because it brought back the same panic. And since now she knew she wasn't imagining things, the horror of what could have happened chilled her soul.

* * *

Vantage Flight 834 landed at Miami three minutes ahead of schedule. The passengers spilled out of the plane into the jetway. Then they poured out into a corridor merging with passengers disembarking from other planes. Everyone was hurrying toward the customs area. No one else noticed the men who drifted into position surrounding two of the passengers from Flight 834.

She noticed, of course. Her heart accelerated, her body tensed preparing for action. But hands on either side firmly clasped her arms and steered her to an obscure door before she had a chance to bolt. Her skin was icy, yet the sweat poured from her, emitting that unique stink of terror. She thought for a minute she would wet her pants, but the moment passed. They moved quickly through the door, down a corridor and through another door. The sun blinded her. The stairs were steep but the grip on her arms did not relax even a fraction. She stumbled, but she wasn't allowed to fall. At the bottom of the stairs she was shoved into the backseat of a car. Her escorts climbed in on either side, two more in front, and the car took off. During this whole time not one word was spoken, yet there was no doubt in anyone's mind what was happening.

The second car containing the man and his escorts, followed the first through the gate onto a service road, and then merged with one of the little used perimeter roads leading from the airport.

"What the hell..." The driver stood on his brakes but couldn't avoid the van, which had careened across their path. The swerving car tossed the passengers into heaps, before crunching into the middle of the van, while the car behind ploughed deeply into their trunk. There was momentary silence with only the brittle sound of broken glass and the screech of rendering metal echoing from all three vehicles. Then quiet settled while the cars' occupants sluggishly opened the doors. The men seemed befuddled by the shock of the accident. They didn't even have time to free their guns from the holsters under their coats before falling under the staccato burst of automatic fire.

The woman stayed huddled on the floor of the backseat. She raised her head when it was quiet once more. She grinned with relief at the familiar faces as she climbed out over bloody corpses.

"Barry?" she inquired simply.

The leader shook his head.

She shrugged. "Let's get out of here."

She headed for the second van, which had pulled out of the driveway. She paused surveying the wreck scattered across the road before climbing into the van.

One of the men tossed something into the wreck and the van took off. The blast behind them seemed to propel the vehicle forward even faster, but no one bothered to look back.

* * *

They were in the conference room waiting for Ames, Fenster, Jack, Harry Greensborough, and Doug Levine. Harry Greensborough, only just arrived from the States, had prompted this meeting. Fenster wasn't quite sure why Doug Levine was there. He was part of State assigned to the Embassy. Usually he kept his distance from the workings of their department unless, of course, he was needed for damage control issues.

Fenster's eyelids were sandpaper and he watched Jack fill his cup with coffee one more time. He wondered how he managed to stay alert. True, his need for a shave and a clean set of clothes was apparent, but his eyes were clear and it was obvious his mind was still working, not just slugging through issues as Fenster felt his had begun to do. Jack was about Fenster's age but, he considered, maybe it had to do with Jack being a field person. He supposed if your life depended on your every action, you would have to be able to stay alert through all kinds of situations.

Fenster realized he was getting soft. He felt slow, dull. But then he too snapped to attention when Ames entered the room, motioning them all to stay seated. Ames was as crisp as a new dollar, looking as if he just arrived after a good night's sleep. Fenster wasn't fooled. He had been in contact with Ames throughout the night and he had always reached him here in his office.

"Good morning, gentlemen. It's been a long night." His eyes swept over the four men at the table, taking in every detail. "Well, Harry, how about bringing us up to date on the situation in Florida."

The news of the capture of Rosa and Barry without incident had been received with glee last evening. Unfortunately, a later dispatch had identified the two cars in the smoldering mass outside the airport grounds as the ones used to transport Rosa and her colleague. That had been a real blow.

"Well, they've recovered three bodies and parts of several others. Presently, they are trying to determine how many and who they are." He looked gravely around the group. "But I think we can safely assume we don't have the one we want."

The other men nodded gravely. Of course. Why else would there have been a smoldering mass, if not to free Rosa?

He continued. "The guesthouse Rosa occupied in California had been very professionally cleaned. We assume Rosa did it before she left, but we got some prints from the main house we haven't yet identified. We're hoping some of those in the main house will be some Rosa overlooked." He shook his head. "I'm not counting on finding anything."

"What about Rosa's luggage? Has it been found?" Jack asked, his frustration obvious.

"It's being checked now." Harry looked at Jack. "I'll make sure they look for DNA on any hair or dandruff sample they can find. We're going to know a lot about Rosa very soon."

"How are the Brits doing with all this?" Doug asked, looking up at last from the papers in front of him. "We have several U.S. citizens here we are concerned about."

Fenster checked the notes he had hastily compiled when he heard Doug was joining them at this meeting. "They've interviewed all the members of the tour, except the four who weren't on the plane. They plan to talk to them when they check-in for the flight home. They feel they can get the information they need and still get them on their plane with no problem." Fenster looked around and then decided to elaborate a bit.

"Actually the Brits have been very cooperative. They, as we, don't want any of the passengers on that plane to know what really happened. They've sent all the other passengers home as soon as possible. The members of our tour have been kept in various hotels, so they won't have a chance to compare information. The Brits and Vantage have been very apologetic about the delay and the interviews have been conducted under the guise of a magazine article on their tour for the *Vantage Vanguard*, the monthly magazine for the passengers. I don't believe the group knows anything about what is going on except what everyone else on the plane thinks. They have all heard about the mechanical failure. They're all very grateful the plane was evacuated. No one on that plane is complaining. They're just so glad about the way the airline is taking care of them."

"Vantage intends to take care of them, and especially Claire Gulliver. I have it straight from their Chairman that she is to be treated very special. In fact, I had to do a lot of talking to convince him it wasn't necessary for him to send a team over to look out for her interests." Doug looked hard at Ames, then swung his eyes to Fenster.

"For Christ sakes, she's at Claridges, sleeping like a baby while two of our guys are watching over her. I think you could safely tell Vantage we're taking care of her adequately." Fenster wished someone cared about his needs. He would be happy for a few hours on the couch in his office.

"Don't mind Fenster, Doug. He hasn't had much sleep and he's disappointed. I'm disappointed. We were so close." He stared straight ahead for a moment, then shook his head slightly. "Well, even if Rosa and Barry got away, we had them. And let's not forget we spoiled their little surprise." He chuckled grimly. "I'll bet they sweat big time when those guys grabbed them in the airport in Miami. They won't be so confident the next time they plan a big hit. And, more importantly, we identified two of them. Rosa will have a sheet. We're going to get fingerprints and maybe DNA from their luggage. It's only a matter of time until we bring them in, and they know it now."

Fenster felt his fatigue lift slightly. That came as close to approval as he ever had from Ames and he was surprised. He was expecting the worst, maybe even a demotion or transfer. Ames did not tolerate failure.

Fenster checked his notes again. "Over half of the passengers have already been sent home on various airlines. Several members of the tour will be included on the first out this morning. None of them will be on the plane later with the four group members who stayed over. We don't want any chance of idle chitchat causing more questions than necessary. The rest of the passengers and everyone on the tour will be out of here by Monday. Except Claire.

"Our colleagues still want more time with Miss Gulliver. They want her deposition on tape and frankly I think that's best. Especially now that we're not sure if Rosa got away. Once that's done, Miss Gulliver will be safer. There won't be any reason for her to have a tragic accident that would prevent her from testifying."

The men nodded. They understood the risks, the need to protect the innocent if they were able.

"Fenster, you make sure Ms. Gulliver has everything she needs. Jack, you stick to her like glue. You know her. She trusts you, doesn't she?"

Jack nodded reluctantly, not wanting to be cut off from the action to be the nanny.

"Doug will want to be there when she is disposed, or whatever they call it here, and then I'm sure Vantage will arrange to get her home comfortably." Ames looked at each man, then concluded, "All right, we meet again here at 1400. All but Jack. Jack you call Fenster with your report. And stay in touch with Doug. He needs to keep Vantage informed and assured that we are acting as they want. We don't want any more fingers in our pie, do we gentlemen?"

They all stood as he left.

Fenster tried to cheer Jack. "Jack, you are the best person to stick to Claire, and it can't be all that bad."

"Bad? Hey, didn't I hear Doug say Vantage wanted her treated special. Get out the monkey suit, Jack. I bet you can do the town. Spare no expense. See all those shows you've been wanting to catch. Am I right, Doug?" Harry wasn't helping.

"Fenster, anybody can guard Claire." Jack tried. Then seeing Fenster's expression he shrugged, turning to Doug.

"Well, Doug, spare no expense?"

Doug nodded. "Vantage will cover it. How long before you think she can leave?"

Fenster paused. "Maybe three to four days, don't you think?"

Harry nodded, and Jack grimaced.

"Okay, I'll keep in touch. Don't forget, I accompany her to any meetings with the Brits."

After he left, Jack looked after him, muttering, "Then why me? Let him look after her." But Fenster and Harry ignored him.

CHAPTER SIXTEEN

Claire came awake slowly, her brain as dim as the room she was in. Not certain where she was or even what time it was, she somehow knew she should be up. Slowly she rolled out of the luxurious bed, her stocking clad feet sank into thick soft carpeting, her clothes rumpled and twisted awkwardly on her body. She headed for the closed door, staggering a little until she found her balance. She had obviously been out a long time. The door opened into a large functional bathroom. And when she noted the basket of amenities waiting on the counter, she recognized immediately she was in a hotel. She went back into the bedroom and looked around. None of her luggage was there. Curious now, she went to the only other door in the room, which opened to a living room.

"Ah, you're alive." Jack looked up from the paper he was reading.

It all came back. She staggered from the hit of memory, grabbing the door jam to steady herself.

"Where are we? How did we get here?" Then noticing the full light in the room, "What time is it?"

"We're at Claridges. And we got here yesterday." He glanced at his watch. "It's now Saturday, 3:15 p.m. You've been asleep about twenty hours."

Claire looked at him with disbelief on her face.

"So how do you feel?" he inquired politely.

She studied him. "Hungry. Yeah, I'm starved. Any chance of getting room service? And my luggage. I need a change of clothes. And I have about a hundred questions.

"Is that today's paper? Is there anything about what happened at the airport? Has anything else happened? Did they catch up with Rosa?"

Jack threw up his hand. "Whoa. Remember I haven't had twenty hours of sleep. I can't keep up with you.

"Your suitcase isn't possible today but maybe tomorrow." He gestured to a pile of bags and boxes on a chair near the bedroom door. "The concierge sent out for those things, perhaps not quite your taste, or size, but they'll probably get you through today."

He gestured to the papers. "Yes, this is today's paper and you're welcome to share it. No, there is nothing in here about what happened at the airport, nor is there likely to be. After all, a newspaper would hardly consider a mechanical failure and a cancellation of a flight as newsworthy, would you think?" He winked at her.

Then his expression hardened. "As for Rosa, we still don't know. We suspect she's gone, but we can't be sure until they finish sorting out the remains of that wreck. We were so sure we had her but she's probably gone. Oh, sure, now we have fingerprints, pictures and we're going to have a DNA profile from the stuff we recovered in her luggage; but we have no clue as to who she is, where she came from or where she will hide."

He rose from the sofa and walked over to a desk holding an ornate phone. He turned back and smiled. "I'll order some food. I feel a little peckish myself. Go ahead and get cleaned up. We'll talk when the food comes."

Rosa was still out there. She most likely would try again. After all that's what terrorists did. Claire shivered, the fear sliding over her. She moved towards the shower, shedding her clothes as she tried to discard her fright. The shower's blast eventually rinsed the haziness from her brain. By the time she stepped out and wrapped herself in the toweling robe hanging on the back of the door, she was remembering the details of what had almost happened.

She admonished herself sharply. "It didn't happen!" But sometimes it was hard to suppress the *what ifs* gnawing at your innards.

She hurried through the rest of her dressing, thinking she was going to have a whole new set of nightmares to contend with. She walked back into the living room as Jack responded to the soft insistent ring of the phone attached to his belt.

"Yes?" He listened a moment then said, "Okay. Thanks." He went to the door and let in a waiter pushing a well-laden cart. The waiter very efficiently turned the cart into a table, spreading out plates of tiny sandwiches, cookies and cakes, and a large dish of strawberries and one of clotted cream. He poured two cups of tea, added cream at Claire's nod and handed her a cup before leaving. Jack accompanied him to the door, securing the lock after him, but not before Claire saw the man stationed in the hall outside.

She moved to a chair close to the tea table, generously filling a plate with the sandwiches. "So, Jack, am I under arrest or something?"

He looked at her quizzically. "What?"

"I saw the man outside. And why are you here? You're not the tour director and I'm sure babysitting isn't on your job description. So?"

She watched him mull this over, but his expression gave no clue as to what he was thinking. He took his time selecting some sandwiches before returning to his seat on the sofa.

"Actually, I am the nanny. You're under protection. We, the guy in the hall, me and several others, are responsible for making sure nothing bad happens to you. We're not sure about this group. We don't know how long their arms are. We don't know how vindictive they might be if they found you were responsible for aborting that flight. After all, we now know they invested months into making this work. And it almost did.

"And as Vantage has obviously credited you with saving their passengers, their airplane, and perhaps, their company, we figured these people may also know about you."

The sandwich turned to sawdust. She spit it into her napkin and drained the cup of tea. She wished she hadn't asked or that she hadn't even noticed. She didn't need to know this.

Jack looked slightly uncomfortable, and he apologized. "I didn't mean to scare you. I just thought you'd rather know the truth."

She nodded.

"Well, we're taking every precaution and after we have all your testimony on tape and all the affidavits signed and secured, we don't anticipate further danger."

"What does that mean? There won't be any danger or you and your buddies won't worry about it?" She couldn't help the sarcastic tone. She felt he was being a little too cavalier about her life. Some of that antagonism she felt toward him when they first met returned.

"Well, there's always the witness protection program for you to consider."

Claire bristled. "So if they do find me, I won't have any family or friends around to know about it? No thanks!"

Jack actually laughed. "I'm sorry. I was just kidding. I shouldn't be giving you a hard time." His face sobered. "If it hadn't been for you that plane would have just disappeared somewhere over the ocean. Can you imagine? We had the tour under surveillance the whole time and if it hadn't been for you, their plan would have worked beautifully.

"What does that say about our abilities to curb terrorist activities?"

They both sat there in silence, thinking about what Jack said. It was scary all right.

"We're all concerned now with your safety, because we don't have enough information to fully evaluate the situation. But once all your testimony is wrapped up, why would anyone want to harm you? These people are fanatics but they usually don't have time for petty vengeance. It's true they wouldn't blink at eliminating someone in their way or someone who is a danger to them. But after your testimony is secured, you will be neither and we expect as safe as you were before.

Claire sat back absorbing this information while she mechanically ate several of the sandwiches. The nightmares she had been having, the bomb ticking, didn't really come from that situation long ago in San Francisco. It had really been her unconscious self warning her of what her conscious mind refused to understand. This was the second time in her life that her intuition had saved her life. Maybe that psychic her friend talked her into visiting was right. She had insisted Claire had special powers and urged her to develop her skills. She told her about some courses in Berkeley, but Claire shrugged it off. She hadn't really believed her. She credited luck for her escape before, but now she wasn't sure.

Suddenly she felt confined. She needed to get some air.

"Jack, what's the agenda here? I'd like to go out and walk. I feel like I've been cooped up for days. Is that a problem?"

Jack seemed a little surprised. "It's probably not a problem as long as you don't mind company."

Jack called someone. Then they went out in the hall where Jack introduced her to Darby, explained the plan to him, and they all went down in the elevator. It was very weird to Claire, having a shadow. He was behind them but unobtrusively. After a while the sunshine, the fresh air and the activity on the streets took her mind off of Darby and whatever it was he was watching for. She felt herself relax when they crossed over into Hyde Park and she stretched out her legs taking long strides, breathing deeply and trying to blank out the past few days.

Gradually, on their way back to the hotel, she and Jack talked about the schedule for the next few days. After a sizable meal from room service, she had a normal night's sleep, no dreams, no nightmares, and woke up ready for her session with the video tape.

* * *

The restaurant was clean, quiet and filled with good smells. Claire looked around at the other diners, a variety people who looked to be locals. Who but locals could have found this spot, tucked in the back of the gourmet market facing the busy street in this posh neighborhood? Doug Levine and Jack conferred over the wine list and then finally decided. The waiter nodding with approval, hurried off to decant their selection. The three of them examined the menu, discussing the merits of various dishes offered. Finally, the wine was poured, the order was placed and they were alone again.

"Well, Claire, congratulations to you. It's over, at least your part, and I would personally like to thank you on behalf of the U.S. Government and especially on behalf of Vantage Airlines." Doug Levine lifted his glass to Claire.

Jack raised his. "I second that. You've done a great job. I'm doubly impressed because these past few days would have worn down most people."

Claire smiled grimly. "You think I haven't been worn down? Worn down, worn out and totally depressed. I'm really anxious to get back to my own world. My bookshop seems so safe, so benign after facing the evils of the world.

"Jack, I just don't know how you can deal with this all the time, how you can keep your sanity."

"Somebody has to do it and that's what keeps me and others like me going. Every little victory, every life saved, gives us the energy to go on." He shook his head. "And it isn't always this bad."

Doug gently changed the subject.

"Claire, the car will be picking you up at 9:00 a.m. Darby is on duty in the morning and will accompany you to the airport and turn you over to Vantages' VIP representative. I understand they're flying you first class, as well they should."

"Is anyone meeting you in San Francisco?" Jack queried.

She shook her head. "Lucy wanted to, but frankly, I just as soon take a taxi. I only live a few miles from the airport and, with all the construction going on there, it's easier than having someone try to pick me up."

"And you're clear about who you can talk to about what?" Jack studied her face carefully.

"Don't worry. I have it all. I have the story for the rest of the tour members and my mother and friends. I know what I can tell Lucy and what I can tell Mrs. B. And, of course, I have all the contact numbers in case I need them." She shuddered. "Which no one thinks will happen, but at least I'm prepared.

"Oh, what about my friend Sean Dixon with the SF Police? If you've been asking a lot of questions he's liable to want to know what's been going on."

Jack and Doug exchanged looks. Then Doug said, "Just tell him whatever he wants to know, as long as you tell him it's confidential."

The waiter discreetly approached with their appetizers, refilling their wine glasses before he left.

"So, Claire, how is it that Sean Dixon is such a fan of yours?" Doug inquired casually as he started to eat.

Claire waved her hand, dismissing the importance as she usually did. "Oh, you know, my father was a police sergeant, so the guys still think they're responsible for seeing I get through life safely."

Doug looked at her thoughtfully. "But it seems more than that. Didn't you tell me, Jack, that he seemed to think Claire could help the Chief Inspector in Conwy when he was investigating Charlie's death?"

Jack nodded, looking at Claire as if to see inside her brain. "Yes, there was something about some drug deal..."

Claire shrugged, giving in. "Well, it was really kind of stupid. I fell into this situation when I agreed to go over to

Ruth's house while she was out of town to take care of her cat. Ruth has been my mother's friend since I was a baby, so it's almost like she's an aunt or something.

"So I went. But the cat got out when I opened the door.

"I was frantic, of course. Ruth thinks that cat is family. I went out on the back deck to see if I could coax her back. I ran the can opener, I banged a spoon on her dish and still no cat. I asked the people sitting out on the deck next door if they had seen her, but they hadn't. So there was nothing to do but go out looking for her.

"I went behind the houses to the park in the back and it was getting quite dark by the time I returned, still without the cat.

"The next thing I knew I had this terrible headache. I was blind. I was cold and I hurt all over. When I finally got my wits about me, I discovered I wasn't really blind. I was somewhere very dark, and I didn't have a clue where I was or how I got there. And I was panicky. I had to get out."

She paused to scrutinize Doug and Jack's faces but found them studying her raptly, so she continued with her story.

"I have this habit of keeping my car keys on a separate chain and stuffing them in my pocket. Of course, my purse was gone and with it my keys and the keys to Ruth's house. But I was lying on my side where the car keys were cutting into my hip, so when I pulled them out I found the little nightlight I keep on the chain. That little light was like a floodlight in the darkness, enough to keep me sane. And when I explored I found I was in what appeared to be a derelict warehouse. The doors were locked but I felt a breeze and following it I found this opening, boarded over, behind some kind of equipment. When I checked it out I could see that someone had broken in before and it had been patched up rather haphazardly.

"Well, as you can imagine, I was confused and scared and desperate to get out. Somehow I got one of the boards pulled out far enough to crawl out.

"But that was almost worse. I didn't know where I was. The section of town I was in was full of warehouses and factories, many of them abandoned. There were very few streetlights and all the shadows seemed grotesque and threatening." She shivered, remembering her terror.

"I was really frightened, and I had this irrational need to get as far as possible from that building I had been in. I started down one street and then another, looking for lights in the distance that would mean other people were around. I don't know how long I wandered, wanting to find help but afraid I'd run into someone. You know what I mean?"

They nodded, caught up in the story, hardly noticing that the waiter removed their plates and brought out their main courses.

"Anyway, finally all the sirens and noises got through to me, and I turned the corner to find a huge fire. Some fire trucks were already there. Others were arriving. As I went closer I realized it was the building I had been in. I could still see the opening where I managed to squeeze out. I had only been wandering in circles.

"Of course, I realized I could have been in there. And the way it was burning it was clear that the firemen were not able to get inside.

"It was too much for me. My legs gave out on me and I sat down on the curb. One of the paramedics found me there. When they took me off to the hospital, they said I had been hit on the head and that was why I couldn't remember."

She stopped to have a few bites of the lamb shank and polenta attractively arranged with baby carrots and green beans on the dish in front of her.

"You're not thinking of stopping this story there are you?" Doug wasn't going to let her get away with that.

"It's just that it's such a long story and frankly it's kind of distressing to go back through all the details. I still have nightmares about it, you know. I think I'm in that warehouse and I wake up screaming for help. It was what was disturbing my sleep on the trip, only with the added feature of the bomb ticking. You know the night before we left I got up and searched the entire room looking for the source of the ticking. But it wasn't there. It was only the dream." She grimaced remembering.

"Okay, not all the details, but you can't leave us hanging. Give us the short version," Jack urged, leaning forward to squeeze her hand encouragingly.

Doug nodded his agreement.

"Well, that's when it's handy to have police officers who think they're your uncles. None of them would even consider I was in that part of town for illicit purposes. So finally they decided I had been mugged. But it kept bothering me. My car was parked down the street from Ruth's house where I had left it that day. Her house was secured and the cat was huddled outside the door, cold, hungry and I'm sure repentant when Ruth returned. I doubt she'll be so anxious for freedom the next chance she has. My purse and my keys were never found."

She sighed, giving up on her meal. Pushing the plate back, she continued. "I got on with my life. I was working in San Francisco at the library, still living with my mother, when the second attempt on my life occurred. We live out in the avenues, on the Richmond side. It was late and I was walking up the hill to our house, when I remembered I was supposed to pick up some milk. I turned around halfway across the street to head back down to the corner store when the car grazed me as it passed. It knocked me down, not that it hit me; it just kind of nudged me off balance, you see?

"I was still getting up when I heard the crash. He was going so fast that when he tried to make the turn at the bottom, he hit the metal utility pole head on. I wasn't hurt, only a few scrapes. But the driver died."

She looked at each of them making sure they understood. "But it was deliberate. It had to be. He didn't have any lights and he was aiming for me. I was on the other side of the street. If I hadn't decided to turn around I would have been imprinted in his grill.

"That really shook me up. Twice within a month is more than I could believe was a coincidence. The police were puzzled but really couldn't help. I decided it was my life at stake, so I had to figure it out."

She smiled. "I was heavily into murder mysteries then. I read every one that came though the library. I could figure out who did it usually after the first couple of chapters. So I figured I would treat this situation as if it was a book. And it helped that the driver of the car seemed vaguely familiar to me. I didn't know him, but I kept feeling I had seen him somewhere.

"Anyway, to shorten this story so we can order dessert, it turned out it was the people on the deck next door to Ruth's house. Some important drug baron was in town and having a meeting. They thought they were safe as they couldn't be seen from the house on the other side, and the owner of the house knew Ruth was out of town. Then I popped out on the deck looking all around. They thought I would recognize them.

She smiled with satisfaction. "And they were right. I could recognize them. When I finally figured out it had to have some connection with Ruth's place, Sean had me go through dozens of books of pictures. I was able to identify three of them.

The police set up a sting and the next time he was in town, they got the whole group. And on top of that, Ruth was so thrilled at being a part of this when they set up her house as a surveillance center, that she forgave me for letting her cat out."

Jack and Doug shook their heads in wonder. "Whew, that's quite a story. No wonder Sean Dixon thought you were so great."

"Well, I have to tell you that little episode changed my life."

"How so?" Doug inquired.

"I've never read another mystery book. They suddenly weren't fun anymore."

They nodded; they could understand that.

"I was always so conservative, cautious with my life. And look what it got me. So I decided I may as well live a little. You know, take a risk. When my uncle left me his bookstore down in the Peninsula, I quit my job, took my retirement monies, moved out from home and started Gulliver's.

"Up to a couple of weeks ago, I've been pleased with myself. But of course, that is what got me on this trip."

"So will you give up on travel?" Doug inquired.

She looked at him. "I don't know. This was my first trip abroad, you know. Jack has tried to convince me, as has Lucy, that this is a very unusual trip, that ordinarily the adventure is much less dangerous." She smiled. "I'll have to think about it. But if I did give up travel books, I don't know what kind of books I would read. I guess I could get into romance novels, but I'm not sure. Gulliver's Romance Bookshop doesn't have the same appeal. Do you think?"

The conversation turned lighter as the waiter cleared their table and took their orders for coffees and desserts. Doug entertained them with a few stories of his experiences in the State Department. Finally, after a discreet phone call on Doug's cell phone, the car was waiting for them out front.

"Need a ride, Jack?" Doug inquired at Claridges.

"No, I need to tuck little Miss Muffet here in, and then go into the office for a bit. Thanks for dinner."

"Little Miss Muffet thanks you too, Doug. And for all the support you've given me during the taping. I appreciate that someone was there for me. Not that anyone was abusive, but you never know where these things are going. I don't have the experience to be confident of handling it all on my own."

She put out her hand, smiling. He took it and leaned in to kiss her on the cheek. "It was my pleasure, Claire. I enjoyed meeting you albeit these circumstances. Maybe some day we'll meet again. I have your address. If I ever get out to California, I'll look you up."

"Please do." She waved one last time and headed for the elevators and her room.

Claire waited in the hall until Jack checked out the suite and called for the guard. He was certainly professional. He gave her the feeling that he knew what he was doing, for a tour guide that is. She smiled to herself at the thought.

"So this is it? You won't be here in the morning?"

He shook his head. "Darby will be with you. We really believe there is no further danger, but we're going to make sure you get on that plane and home safely."

He stood in front of her, holding her shoulders, peering intently into her face. Then he leaned in to kiss her softly.

"I'll miss you. I think I've grown fond of you. But I'm glad it's over. Maybe some day we'll meet again." He smiled.

She nodded, returning his smile as he closed the door behind him. He was right. It was over and she could finally relax.

* * *

When Jack and Fenster entered the briefing room it was full. They nodded at Nigel Smythe-Cook and Ian Flemming before taking seats as close to the front as possible. Fenster nodded to several other colleagues, and introduced himself to some he didn't recognize. Jack sat quietly. In his position it was better not to know or be known by too many people in the business. In fact, he was a little surprised he had been included in this briefing of the results of the tests of Rosa's suitcase. But it was probably because he was the only one of them who had actually had contact with her.

"Gentlemen and ladies." Ames nodded to the few women present. "I thought it would be appropriate to meet and share all the information we have been able to glean about our suspect, Rosa Morino."

The screen behind him flashed through the pictures they had of Rosa, including the one taken at passport control at Heathrow.

"Of course, we know her name is not Rosa Morino. The real Rosa was found two days ago in a heavily wooded area between her house and the airport. The car she ordered to take her there, didn't."

He paused while everyone imagined the real Rosa's last trip to the airport. Then he introduced the two experts from the States who had analyzed the luggage retrieved from the Vantage Florida flight.

During the next half hour the experts led them through a series of findings, including fingerprints, DNA findings and characteristics described by witnesses.

"The DNA proves without a doubt that Rosa is a he, not a she. But apparently he is an invisible one. We have not been able to identify him. How he could have existed without being fingerprinted is beyond our comprehension.

"However, this leads us to believe he may be the man. He may be the elusive Guiness we have all sought."

The stunned silence built to a roar as conversations broke out and questions were asked.

The speaker held out his hands gesturing for silence. "We know this is big news, but bear with us for a while and then we'll take questions and suggestions.

"We have had our artists prepare pictures of what he may look like, based on the measurement of his features. We're assuming he kept his disguise as simple as possible, because the close proximity of living at Lucy's and joining the tour would make maintaining a complex makeup job too risky. We know Rosa used heavy pancake makeup, probably to hide the five o'clock shadow. And the eye makeup and lipstick was styled after the sixties. The high collars and scarf she wore were probably used to hide a prominent Adam's apple.

"We have no clue of his actual age. The only reason we're looking to Ireland is because that's the source of years of rumors of his existence. But of course, he could be Canadian, American, English or from any country. His language is very good. He passed as an American woman for several months. What does that tell you?"

Fenster's assistant passed out kits containing pictures and data. And as the attendees were looking through them, the speakers did their best to answer the detailed questions put to them.

Jack listened with half an ear while he scrutinized the pictures, amazed at how different the suspect looked as a man.

Ames took the lead again. “Well, people, this is the most we’ve ever gotten on Guiness. We are forming an international task force to track him. We are starting to know him. He is resourceful. He is bold. He is utterly without conscience.

“And for a while he is going to be careful. He knows we almost had him. He is the only person to walk away from that wreck outside of the Miami airport. He knows we now have information we have never had before. But that won’t stop him. Our psychiatric profilers believe he considers himself invincible and that, Gentlemen and Ladies, that is how we’re finally going to get him.”

Claire let herself in the front door, stepping immediately back in time. The smells, the feel and even the furniture were straight out of her childhood, albeit long past.

"Is that you dear?" her mother called from the kitchen.

"Of course, who else has a key?" Claire gave her mother a hug and a kiss on the cheek. "Something sure smells good." She couldn't stop herself from peeking in the oven. "Yum, macaroni and cheese."

Her mother smiled. "All your favorites to celebrate your return and to keep you happy while you tell me all about your trip. Do you have your pictures yet?

"I have a white wine in the refrigerator, if you want to pour it. Dinner will be ready in about twenty minutes."

Claire did that and then sat down at the kitchen table already laid with the cheerful dinnerware. She stared out the window to the fog-shrouded back yard. It was summer in San Francisco and that meant fog in the Avenues. It usually burned off sometime during the day only to return again in the evening. This little house had been built as a summer cottage before the turn of the century, as were four other houses, perched on the steep hill up to Geary. The rest of the block housed four or six unit apartment buildings, built to use every square inch of the lot they sat on.

Claire remembered how the bulldozers came after each property sold and how the street started changing. Now there were only a few holdouts. And when her mother decided to sell, the buyer would most likely triple his investment by building multiple units.

When she was a child, she knew everyone on the block. This house was her haven of safety. Even during that terrible time after her father was killed, her mother somehow kept this house inviolate. Now, she knew that an insurance policy paid off the house and a pension contributed to their well being. But still her mother took a part time job in the bookkeeping department of the local Cadillac franchise. Claire owed her mother a lot. She may have been cautious, overly cautious as some said, but Claire grew up safe, secure and feeling very loved. She understood now, as an adult, how much her mother must have given up to make that all happen.

Her mother interrupted her reminiscing when she set out the baking dish of macaroni and cheese, along with the salad and fresh rolls. Then seated she took a sip of her wine and sighed. "Well, you look great, rested and, I don't know, maybe energized. I guess this trip was good for you?"

Claire nodded. "It was wonderful, Mom. Really, you should do it." She helped herself liberally to the food and then started telling her edited story, making much of some of the funny incidents, like the head to head confrontation with the beer lorry on the road to Conwy and Mrs. Maus taking over grouchy Joe.

They had both stopped eating by the time Claire got to Liz's broken collarbone and Arnie's accident. Her mother was horrified.

"Claire, it sounds really dangerous. How could someone fall off a wall?" She shook her head. "I didn't realize it would be dangerous. If I had, I would have worried the whole time you were gone."

"Now, Mom, you know you worried the whole time anyway." She smiled waiting for her mother's agreement. "It wasn't dangerous. Really. And Arnie's accident was very unusual. You know that the police in Conwy didn't know how it happened.

"And we all walked the wall in York, even Mrs. Maus with her cane. We had a really great time. You need to go yourself. All the books and travel films can't even come close to being there yourself."

"Well, my church ladies have been pressuring me to join them on a cruise to Alaska. And, I admit, I'm tempted."

Claire jumped at it. "That would be so great. You'd have fun. I've heard that Alaska is incredibly beautiful. And those cruises are so romantic.

"Why don't you? You can afford it."

"Well, you know I don't like to touch that money for frivolous things. It's an emergency fund."

"Mom, you're close to retirement. You need some excitement in your life. Take a chance and live a little. Talk to Ruth about it."

"Oh, I can't talk to her about it. You know she'd tell me to go and do it, spend it all. You know how she is."

"Yes, and it's not a bad life, you know. She goes everywhere and has a great time. It would do you good to try a little."

"Well, I'll think about it. Meanwhile, I have to say it's a relief to have you back. I know I don't see you all the time now that you're down on the Peninsula, but I know just where you are, and I can talk to you every day. I didn't like it that you were on the other side of the world."

Claire nodded, patting her mother's arm. They might annoy each other sometimes, but they were very close, dependant on each other. And right now Claire was very relieved she got through the story of the trip without letting anything slip that shouldn't have. It was hard to lie to her mother—well, not lie really, but omit. Was omission the same as lying?

"You should get the details of that cruise, Mom, maybe the brochure. Who would you room with?"

Her mother waived off the details. "I'll think about it and we'll talk later. There's plenty of time. It's not planned until late next spring."

"Okay, but give it some serious consideration. And talk to Ruth.

"Oh, I brought you a few things. Just a minute and I'll get them." She jumped up and retrieved the bags she dropped in the living room when she arrived, smiling with anticipation of her mother's reaction to the presents she chose for her.

* * *

"All right, Claire, we've gone over every little thing that went on while you were gone. So now it's your turn. Cough up the details. I need to hear it all."

"Let's move to the alcove and get comfy. Do you want a Coke, or a glass of wine?"

Mrs. B took a Coke from the little refrigerator they kept in the backroom. Claire filled a glass with Chardonnay, knowing she needed some fortification for the telling of this tale.

The store had closed at eight and now only the alcove was dimly lit and inviting. They settled themselves in two old wingback chairs and Claire started her story at the end, determined to get the worst over first.

Mrs. B paled visibly when Claire told about accosting the stewardesses and insisting the plane be stopped. She had to set her glass down on the little table next to her because her hand was shaking as Claire told about the plane evacuation and her transport to the little waiting room. And she gasped when Claire told her the bomb had been found.

She opened her mouth several times but nothing came out. She was so shocked, Claire was feeling guilty, wondering why she had been so sure she had to tell her the whole story.

Finally, "I never liked her," she muttered.

"I beg your pardon?" Claire couldn't quite hear her.

"I never liked her. There was something about her that just made me uncomfortable." Mrs. B said strongly, more like her old self. "I just can't take this all in, Claire. You could have been...

"You all would have..." She swallowed and tears sprang to her eyes. "And here I was urging you to go."

She groped in her pocket for the hanky she always carried, wiping at her eyes. "I'm such a fool. I almost got you killed." And she completely broke down, sobbing in anger at her own stupidity.

"Oh, Mrs. B. It's not your fault. You have no blame. Rosa's to blame. Only Rosa. Both you and Lucy were right to urge me to go. It was the right thing to do, and I did have a wonderful time. We all did. How were any of us to know? Who would have thought that there would be so much evil, so much treachery?"

Claire knelt beside Mrs. B's chair and put her arms around her, hugging her. "It wasn't your fault, truly. Why would you think that something like this would happen?

We just wouldn't think that way, and we don't want to think that way, do we?"

Mrs. B stopped sobbing and looked at Claire. "No, no. But I feel so guilty."

Claire patted her fondly. "Don't, it wasn't your fault. I don't blame you, so don't you blame yourself. I don't know what I'd do if you stopped urging me to do new and different things. What if you let me revert to that cautious, timid librarian I was for so many years? You've been very good for me and to me. Don't stop now.

"Don't let Rosa win!"

Mrs. B smiled, somewhat shaky, but a smile nonetheless. She took a sip of her soft drink, sighed and then looked at Claire. "Okay, now tell me the rest, the fun part."

They talked way too late into the night, but they knew the shop would be closed the next day and they could sleep late. Claire wanted to tell her everything and Mrs. B was determined to hear it all.

By the time they each headed for home, Mrs. B, recovering somewhat from her shock, had agreed that she would never, ever, ever, ever let a word of Rosa's treachery escape from her lips. And especially, she promised to never let Claire's mother have a clue of the danger her daughter had been in. Claire was relieved. Somehow sharing the details with Lucy and Mrs. B had released some of the terror she kept inside since that awful day. She was truly lucky to have such good friends.

* * *

"Here you go, Lucy." Teri handed her the cup of tea, then returned to get one for herself.

Lucy thanked her, setting the tea on the table next to her chair. She was pleased she could get around much easier now that she had exchanged the plaster cast for a smaller Velcro and plastic one. She only needed her cane to steady herself. Still, as soon as she arrived, she had planted herself in one of the comfy chairs in the alcove not wanting to stand for long. She loved this section of Claire's shop. It was almost like having your own library.

She watched Claire, who stood near the entrance, welcome the members of the tour as they arrived. She was so relieved Claire was so forgiving about sending her off on that tour from hell. She wasn't sure she would have been so understanding. In fact, considering how she felt about Rosa, she was sure she wouldn't have been.

Claire was pleased so many of the tour members had made it back to the reunion. Liz wasn't there, of course, because Claire hadn't invited her. Right or not, she didn't want to deal with her. But she was glad to know her collarbone was healing nicely and that she had taken a job as an assistant to a professor at the University in Santa Barbara. According to Lucy, she was in the process of moving down the coast and she was energetic and acting very positive. Claire hadn't wanted to test that by having her at the reunion, although technically she was one of the alumni.

The Mohney's were in Michigan for the rest of the summer and regretted that they wouldn't have a chance to see everyone's pictures.

Betty hadn't come. Claire had talked to her on the phone and she said she was improving, finally. She thanked Claire again for all her efforts in getting her home and for not revealing her tragedy. But she just wasn't up to seeing everyone right now. She said maybe she'd come to the next one.

Of course Arnie wasn't there.

And Rosa wouldn't be there.

Everyone else was there. They passed around pictures. They shared memories and stories. They drank the tea Claire provided, just happy to be together again.

"Joe, you're looking well."

Joe beamed. "Got a job, you know."

Claire couldn't hide her surprise. She thought he had been retired for quite a while. "A job? What are you doing?"

"I'm working over at the senior center with Maureen. I'm helping the cook. They love my marinara sauce." He seemed inordinately pleased with himself. He lowered his voice. "I swear I didn't realize, Claire, how hard it is for many of the seniors to exist with only their Social Security checks. They don't get enough to eat and pay rent. So the lunch the Senior Center provides almost free five times a week is really a worthwhile cause."

Claire nodded, agreeing with him, but amazed at the change. "But Joe, isn't this a long way to come every day? Couldn't you do something similar up in the City?"

He nodded. "But I moved in with my son's family last weekend. I decided I was too young to hang around with those old farts in the park playing bocce ball. I still have a little juice in me. I still have a few things that I can teach my grandkids, you know?"

Vern came up and put his arm around her. "How's our intrepid leader? Recovered from all that traveling?"

"Hey, Vern, did you hear that Joe moved down to live with his son?"

Vern beamed and clapped Joe lightly on the back. "Good for you. Going to be a little closer to Mrs. Maus, huh?"

Claire was amused to see that Joe could blush.

Mike and Alice joined them, Mike announcing, "Did Vern tell you that we're going to Paris?"

They looked at him with surprise.

"Yep, we're wondering why we've wasted all this time. You'll see us here poring through the books on Paris, and we'll probably even buy a few."

Everyone laughed.

Vern nodded his agreement. "We're spending Christmas in Paris."

Glenda and Alex joined them, then Kim and Warren. Everyone had suggestions for Vern and Mike's trip to Paris.

Claire separated herself and wandered across the room to the teapot. She overheard Shar ask Lucy how she was getting the book finished now that Rosa had left for another emergency assignment. She paused, eavesdropping, glad Lucy had to field that question and not her.

"Oh, that was inconvenient, but I really did understand Rosa's position. After all, she had gathered all the data I needed, so really anyone could do the editing and final changes. And this was someone she owed her loyalty to. She had worked for him several times in the past. So I have a very efficient young man from the temporary agency working on it, and it looks like we'll meet our schedule without a problem."

She smiled, looking calm and serene, not at all worried. That was all an act. Lucy had been livid and then frantic when she learned there was no data, no confirmation of prices, no checks on the various opening hours that she needed. If Rosa had actually done any checking, she had not recorded it. And most likely there had been no checking. Liz had been absolutely correct. Rosa had spent her time meeting with her colleagues, collecting pieces she needed and building her bomb.

It had been Claire's suggestion for Lucy to contract with Kingdom Coach Tours to have someone follow their route and verify the data. That was costly but it worked. And the information was obtained in a minimum of time. So, it was true the young man from the temporary agency was finishing up the revisions and the first half of the book had already been submitted to Lucy's publisher. In fact, the next time the group met it would probably be at Lucy's book launch party scheduled in the early part of next year.

"Claire," whispered Joan, approaching with Mary. "Mary wants to tell you something." She smiled smugly.

Mary blushed, smiled and nodded. "I'm expecting. Probably about the time Lucy's book is launched."

"Oh, Mary, how great! Are John and the kids excited?"

"Well John, is. We haven't told the kids yet. We're waiting until I start showing."

"I guess John will think again about the next vacation he wants to take without the kids, huh, Mary? See what happens when you leave the kids at home?" Joan could barely suppress her laughter.

"I'm sure it was that tea dance." Mary confided, "It was just too romantic."

They couldn't help it. The giggles took over.

Claire whispered to Mary, "Be sure and tell Lucy. She'll be so happy for you."

Shar turned their way. "What are you all whispering and giggling about? Come on and share it with the rest of us."

The three looked at each other and nodded. "Okay, Shar, here's the news."

It didn't take long to get through the entire room, and Lucy had to raise her voice to get everyone's attention. "Well, here's to our next meeting. We'll have my book, Mary's and John's baby, and Vern and Mike's pictures from

Paris. I think we can all say that this Armchair Adventure was a success. Thank you all for being a part of it."

The cheers from the alcove reverberated through the bookshop startling browsers, who looked up from their books to gaze at the alcove with curiosity.

EPILOGUE

Going through the mail was never Claire's favorite task, so the plate of ginger snaps and the mug of tea were meant as a bribe. She dutifully sorted the accumulation in the basket until she reached the heavily embossed envelope from Vantage Airlines. She felt a clutch of fear grip her stomach as she turned it over, examining it carefully.

It was strange how quickly things had returned to normal after she came back from London. The story for the other tour members and her mother and friends was readily accepted. Why not? No one would have guessed what really happened.

Of course, Lucy, Mrs. B and Claire all knew the truth and were haunted by *what had almost* happened. But then as the weeks passed, and they became once more involved in the details of every day life, those fears gradually receded.

Claire studied the creamy stationery. This was no normal promotional offer, she could tell. She used her letter opener to cut through the top and unfolded the letter to scan the contents. She read it a second time more carefully.

The CEO and President, David Burlington Lickman was inviting her to be Vantage's guest in Washington DC. She was invited to attend a special meeting of the Board, so they could show their appreciation for her efforts on behalf of their corporation. Additionally, the Lickmans would like her to be their guest for the long Labor Day weekend in their home in Maryland, where they were hosting a gala to celebrate the end of the summer.

She was stunned. Who would expect a major corporation such as Vantage Airlines to issue such a personal invitation? She thought it was a really caring thing to do. It made her feel like they really did appreciate what she had done. She decided right then that the Lickmans must be very nice people.

But she really felt a little guilty about Vantage's appreciation. Truthfully, she hadn't given a thought to saving the airline. She had been totally concerned with her own safety and that of the others on the plane. The results of course benefited them all. Doug Levine, who had been the State Department's representative assigned to protect her interests through all the interrogation and investigations by the British, had kept telling her how grateful the airline was for her action. That had planted an expectation in her head that she could expect some formal thank you and perhaps even a gesture of appreciation, like some free bonus miles or a complimentary ticket to somewhere. But then as the weeks passed without hearing from Vantage, she had dismissed the idea. But never had she expected a personal invitation such as this.

Yes, she admitted, she had always wanted to see Washington DC. She had vowed someday she would go to the Vietnam Memorial, because she identified so much with that era while she was growing up in San Francisco. And she had heard so much about the Smithsonian. It would probably take a week to even make a dent in the museums. And of course, what librarian (albeit ex-librarian) could resist an opportunity to visit the Library of Congress?

She toyed with the idea of getting on a plane again. It was so soon. She kind of rolled it around a bit in her mind, but strangely the thought didn't seem to alarm her. What did concern her was her business. She had a bookstore to run and it needed her. She couldn't just be running off on trips every few months.

A gala, she thought. What was that precisely? It sounded rather posh. She decided to ask Lucy about it. Lucy, her travel book author friend, was the one who knew just what Claire should wear when she had been invited to an afternoon society wedding several months back. Surely she would know what a gala required, and maybe she had even heard of the Lickmans. Or, she thought, she could check the Web. David Lickman, as the head of a major corporation, could surely be found on Google.

She was tempted by the invitation. Maybe she'd discuss the trip with Mrs. B, her assistant manager, when she came in this afternoon. Maybe there was a way. Maybe it was possible. It seemed that this was a unique opportunity, something not to be missed.

And Labor Day was only a month away.

If you enjoyed this book, or any other book from Koenisha Publications, let us know. Visit our website or drop a line at:

Koenisha Publications
3196 – 53rd Street
Hamilton, MI 49419
Phone or Fax: 269-751-4100
Email: koenisha@macatawa.org
Web site: www.koenisha.com

Coming Soon
The sequel to *Tea is for Terror*
Washington Weirdos
by Gayle Wigglesworth

Koenisha Publications authors are available for speaking engagements and book signings. Send for arrangements and schedule or visit our website.

Purchase additional copies of this book from your local bookstore or visit our web site.

Send for a free catalog of titles from
KOENISHA PUBLICATIONS
Founder of the Jacketed SoftCover™
Books You Can Sink Your Mind Into